A HEARTFELT NOTE

EMBARKING THE PATH TO PARENTHOOD.......

SAKUNTHALA SANTOSH

Copyright © Sakunthala Santosh
All Rights Reserved.

This book has been self-published with all reasonable efforts taken to make the material error-free by the author. No part of this book shall be used, reproduced in any manner whatsoever without written permission from the author, except in the case of brief quotations embodied in critical articles and reviews.

The Author of this book is solely responsible and liable for its content including but not limited to the views, representations, descriptions, statements, information, opinions and references ["Content"]. The Content of this book shall not constitute or be construed or deemed to reflect the opinion or expression of the Publisher or Editor. Neither the Publisher nor Editor endorse or approve the Content of this book or guarantee the reliability, accuracy or completeness of the Content published herein and do not make any representations or warranties of any kind, express or implied, including but not limited to the implied warranties of merchantability, fitness for a particular purpose. The Publisher and Editor shall not be liable whatsoever for any errors, omissions, whether such errors or omissions result from negligence, accident, or any other cause or claims for loss or damages of any kind, including without limitation, indirect or consequential loss or damage arising out of use, inability to use, or about the reliability, accuracy or sufficiency of the information contained in this book.

Made with ♥ on the Notion Press Platform
www.notionpress.com

To my incredible family, supportive husband, and cherished friends, your constant encouragement and unwavering belief in my abilities fueled the journey of completing my book. Your inspiration is the ink that flows through the pages of my creative endeavors. Thank you for being my muse and my steadfast cheerleaders. Special thanks to Jayasree Menon a friend of mine who designed the cover picture and to my mentor Santosh Satyamoorthy, for transforming my dream of becoming an author into a reality.

Dedicated to my incredible family, supportive husband, and cherished friends; within the symphony of my creative journey, the steadfast support and continuous encouragement from my family have functioned as the harmonious melody that propelled the completion of this book. The inspiration drawn from each family member permeates the ink on these pages, shaping my thoughts into tangible words. They are not merely cheerleaders but pillars, steadfast and supportive, upon which this literary endeavor firmly rests. The dedication is extended to each family member for being the driving force behind my creativity and unwavering advocates of my dreams.

Special thanks to Jayasree Menon, a dear friend whose artistic talent graces the cover of this book. Her visual interpretation adds another layer of depth to the story within.

To my mentor, Santosh Iyer, your guidance has been invaluable in turning the dream of becoming an author into a tangible reality. His influence echoes in every word, shaping this narrative.

Contents

Contents

Preface

In this vast expanse of literature, we find ourselves entangled in a situation faced by today's young generation. The chapters are marked by heartfelt sacrifices with pulsating dreams. Within these pages, one can find tales that delve into the struggles of couples yearning to become parents.

The narratives unfold the delicate dance between societal norms and personal dreams, exploring the emotional complexities of these intimate journeys. These stories serve as an ode to the relentless human spirit, offering a glimpse into the challenges, resilience, and the profound joy that can arise from such struggles.

Let these tales resonate, inspire, and provoke introspection as you partake in the multifaceted events experienced by a family.

Welcome to a journey through the written word – a journey that transcends time, space, and the boundaries of imagination, inviting you to explore the intricate canvas painting of human experiences.

Prologue

In the ever-evolving palette of life, where the hues of fate intertwine, there lies a story of resilience, love, and the indomitable spirit of Vinaya and Vijay. Seasoned IT professionals who once seamlessly navigated the intricacies of the digital realm, they now find themselves standing at the threshold of an unparalleled adventure—the pure and uncharted territories of parenthood.

As Vinaya and Vijay embark on this extraordinary journey, they do so hand in hand, drawing strength from the unbreakable bond that has weathered storms and celebrated triumphs. Their shared goal echoes in the corridors of their hearts—a commitment to provide the utmost care and a nurturing environment for their little one to flourish.

Yet, the path that led them to this juncture was not a smooth one. The couple faced the formidable challenge of infertility, a maze of complexities that tested the limits of their emotional endurance. Together, with the unwavering support of their families, they navigated the twists and turns of conception, confronting the heartbreak of an abortion, and bravely embracing the subsequent struggles that followed after bringing their child into the world.

Through the highs and lows, Vinaya and Vijay's commitment to each other remained steadfast. Their journey is a testament to the resilience born out of love—a love that transcends the trials of life, emerging even stronger in the face of adversity. As they step into the realm of pure parenthood, their story unfolds as a captivating narrative of hope, courage, and the transformative power of enduring love.

Acknowledgements

I would like to express my deepest gratitude to my family, whose unwavering support has been the cornerstone of my journey to becoming an author. Their love, encouragement, and understanding have been my constant companions throughout this fulfilling endeavor.

A special appreciation goes to my husband, Santosh Iyer whose patience, belief, and encouragement have been my pillars of strength. His steadfast support and belief in my dream have been instrumental in turning it into reality. His insights, constructive feedback, and encouragement have played a pivotal role in shaping my writing and refining my storytelling skills.

I am also profoundly thankful to Jayasree Menon, whose creativity crafted the cover page of this book.

I extend my heartfelt thanks to the teachers who have inspired and influenced me along the way. Their passion for education and dedication to nurture the creativity within me has left an indelible mark on my writing style and approach. Each of them has contributed to my growth as an author.

To my readers, I extend my sincere appreciation for embracing my work. Your support and enthusiasm fuel my motivation to continue exploring new realms of storytelling. I am profoundly grateful to all those who have been part of this incredible journey. Thank you for being a part of this chapter in my life.

CHAPTER ONE

THE UNSPOKEN REALITIES

The moon cast a gentle glow over the night, illuminating the room where Vijay and Vinaya found solace away from the prying eyes of their family. As they isolated themselves, a heavy silence hung in the air, laden with the weight of unspoken fears and uncertainties.

Vijay sighed, the weight of impending parenthood pressing on his shoulders like an invisible burden. "Vinaya," he began, his voice tinged with hesitation, "have you noticed how our families keep dropping not-so-subtle hints about us having kids? It's as if they've already decided for us."

Vinaya nodded, her eyes reflecting the same concern. "Yes, Vijay. Every family gathering turns into a subtle interrogation about our plans for children. It's like they believe that, it's the only path to happiness. But I can't help feeling a sense of anxiety about it all. It's not that simple."

Vijay's hands trembled with a mix of frustration and despair as he forcefully ran his fingers through his hair. The room seemed to close in on him, the weight of unspoken expectations and societal pressure bearing down like an oppressive force.

"I get it," he exhaled, the words laced with a palpable tension. It's not that I don't want to be a father, but these expectations are suffocating me," he confessed, his voice strained with the raw emotion of the moment.

The air in the room hung heavy with the unspoken turmoil, as if the very walls were privy to the unrelenting pressure Vijay felt. They talk about the joys of parenthood, but what about the challenges? What about our dreams and aspirations?"

Vinaya leaned against the window, staring into the night. "Exactly. It's like they've romanticized the idea of having kids without considering the complexities. And every time they bring it up, I feel this invisible clock ticking, reminding me that time is slipping away."

Smitha, with a demeanor softer than a whisper, delicately stepped into the circle of their solitude. "No one is going to reveal the web of difficulties that come with parenting," Sorry that I overheard your conversations; she murmured, her words a soothing balm for the restless souls of Vijay and Vinaya.

In the stillness of that moment, Smitha, a seasoned voyager in the realm of parenthood, revealed the concealed truths — the sleepless nights that morph into endless worry, the sacrifices etched in the silence of selfless love. The world, charmed with the scenic idea of having children, was blissfully ignorant of the harsh realities that wove the fabric of the unspoken narrative of parenthood.

"People around you," Smitha continued, her voice like a calm gentle wind, "they only want to revel in the joy of having kids. Are they going to shoulder the burdens of your sleepless nights? No! They come, they smile, they cuddle with your little one, and then they depart. That's the script the aunts and people in the societies follow. So, you both, chill," she reassured, as if laying a comforting hand on their anxious hearts. Her voice carried the weight of experience, a reminder that the journey ahead was uniquely theirs to navigate.

Vijay and Vinaya exchanged glances, the gravity of Smitha's words settling upon them like a profound realization. Parenthood, they now understood, was not a mere collection of joyous moments frozen in time, but an intricate abstract art, painted with hues of time and patience. Smitha's wisdom resonated within them, urging them to unravel the layers of societal expectations and carve out a path uniquely their own.

"Becoming a parent is an expedition that demands time and patience," Smitha continued, her eyes fixed on the horizon of the impending journey. "So, both of you must understand... embarking on parenthood is not about conforming to what others say. It's about discerning what you truly want.

" And so, with those words, the first chapter of Vijay and Vinaya's unwritten novel — a novel that would unfold with each passing day, a blank canvas painted with laughter and tears, triumphs and tribulations. Societal norms and expectations were cast aside as they embraced the distinct challenges and joys that parenthood held for them.

As the couple stood hand in hand, they embarked on this uncharted journey, ready to script their own narrative and redefine the very essence of parenthood on their own terms.

Little did they know that the most profound lessons were often concealed in the silent spaces between the lines, where the intricacies of life's novel awaited discovery, eager to be unfolded in the pages of their shared destiny.

CHAPTER TWO

LIFE -THE JOURNEY WITH SACRIFICES

In the quaint remote industrial area named Krishnapattanam, at Hyderabad, Manju and Sidharth led a simple yet fulfilling life. Their cozy home was surrounded by industries, where opportunities were in abundance. Sidharth worked diligently as a General Manager in the village's chemical factory, while Manju dedicated herself to managing the household and raising their two sons, Varun and Vijay.

One evening, as the sun gracefully descended below the horizon, painting the sky with a vibrant array of colors and casting a gentle, warm glow upon Krishnapattanam, Manju and Sidharth sat on the porch, reflecting on the choices that had sculpted their lives.

Sidharth sighed, looking at Manju with a mixture of gratitude and concern. "You know, Manju, sometimes I wonder if we made the right decision. You gave up your career for the kids, for us."

Manju, gazing into the distance, smiled softly.

"Sidharth, it wasn't a sacrifice. It was a choice. I wanted our sons to have the best upbringing, to feel the warmth of a loving home. My career could wait, but their childhood couldn't."

Sidharth took Manju's hand in his, tracing the lines of time that had etched their story. "But, my love, you had dreams too. What about your ambitions?"

Manju turned to Sidharth, her eyes reflecting the depth of her commitment. "My ambition was to see our boys grow into good, compassionate human beings. And look at them now, successful, responsible. I have no regrets."

As the boys entered adulthood, excelling in their studies and securing jobs, Sidharth couldn't help but express his gratitude. "Manju, you were right. Our boys are thriving, and it's all because of you. I might be the General Manager at the factory, but you're the real architect of our family's success."

Manju blushed; her humility evident in her response. "We did it together, Sidharth. Our partnership, our love, that's what made it all possible."

The pivotal moment materialized when Varun, the elder son, discovered love in Smitha, a skilled general physician at a renowned hospital who eventually established a clinic in Krishnapattanam. Observing the blossoming romance, Sidharth turned to Manju with a twinkle in his eye. "Our boy is coming of age. He's found someone truly special."

Manju chuckled, "Yes, and it warms my heart to see him happy. Smitha will be a wonderful addition to our family."

Varun and Smitha's union became the heartwarming spectacle of Krishnapattanam. The village embraced their love with a lavish celebration, where joy echoed through every corner. The air was filled with laughter and the infectious rhythm of celebratory music, as the entire village came together to honor the graceful couple.

The wedding venue was adorned with vibrant colors, floral arrangements, and the rich cultural palette of Krishnapattanam. The aroma of traditional delicacies wafted through the air, teasing the senses and adding to the festive ambiance.

Villagers, dressed in their finest attire, gathered to witness the union of Varun and Smitha; a union that symbolized not just the coming together of two individuals but the merging of families and the continuation of a legacy.

Varun, in his traditional attire, stood with a beaming smile as Smitha, adorned in resplendent bridal attire, walked towards him with grace and poise. The exchange of vows was accompanied by the sacred chants, resonating with the blessings of the elders and the warmth of the community. The couple, surrounded by loved ones, embarked on a journey that promised a lifetime of shared dreams and companionship.

Happiness radiated from Varun and Smitha's faces as they partook in the festivities. The rhythmic beats of traditional drums merged with the joyous laughter of the villagers, creating a symphony of celebration. The couple, hand in hand, participated in traditional rituals that bound them together not only in the eyes of their families but in the hearts of the entire village.

The festivities continued late into the night, with a grand feast that showcased the culinary delights of Krishnapattanam.

The graceful couple, still wearing the glow of newlyweds, moved through the crowd, thanking well-wishers and sharing heartfelt moments with friends and family.

As the night unfolded, the village square transformed into a dance floor, and the twinkling stars above seemed to join the celebration. Varun and Smitha, surrounded by the love and blessings of Krishnapattanam, danced under the moonlit sky, symbolizing the beginning of a new chapter filled with love, companionship, and the promise of a blissful future. The lavish village wedding of Varun and Smitha became a cherished memory etched into the collective heart of Krishnapattanam, a testament to the enduring power of love and community.

As Vijay, the younger son, found his life partner in Vinaya, the family continued to grow. Manju and Sidharth, now witnessing the joyous occasions of their sons' marriages, held onto each other, finding comfort in the legacy they had built.

Manju, reflecting on their journey, whispered to Sidharth, "The sacrifices were worth it, weren't they?"

Sidharth nodded, his eyes filled with pride and love. "More than worth it. They were the building blocks of this beautiful life we have."

The legacy of love, sacrifice, and values passed down from Manju and Sidharth continued to thrive through Varun and Vijay's families.

The village of Krishnapattanam now stood as a testament to the power of a family's love, echoing the sentiment that sometimes, the most profound stories unfold in the simplest of settings.

This was just the beginning; a palette with multiple hues of experiences that awaited the families. As they pondered the unknown chapters ahead, the echoes of Manju and Sidharth's conversations lingered, a reminder that love and sacrifice were the cornerstones of their enduring legacy.

CHAPTER THREE

HUES OF LOVE – THE BEGINNING

A year had elapsed since the delighted parents, lovingly referred to as Dada and Amma, basked in the joy of their two sons and their families. Varun, the elder son, and his wife Smitha, alongside their daughter Suma, the recent addition to the family, constituted one cornerstone of this ideal joint family. Meanwhile, the younger son, Vijay, and his wife Vinaya, contributed another layer of happiness to this blissful ensemble.

The house, a haven of laughter and shared moments, echoed with the innocence and mischievous actions of the little one. The walls bore witness to the silly fights and the joyous celebrations that marked the colored palette of their lives. Love, the invisible hue that painted through each interaction, created a vibrant realistic painting of familial bonds.

Varun and Smitha, the seasoned elders, guided their child with wisdom and warmth. The mischievous giggles and the innocent laughter of Suma brought an added glow to their lives. Vijay and Vinaya, the younger couple, radiated the energy of love that was still in the bloom of its youth. Together, they created a symphony of love, where every member played a unique note, contributing to the melody of their shared existence.

As the sun descended beneath the horizon, it covered the family in a soothing, warm radiance; a significant decision took root in the hearts of Vijay and Vinaya. The bustling city of Mumbai beckoned, promising new horizons and unexplored dreams. They decided to chase their aspirations, armed with determination and each other's unwavering support.

Vijay: (standing at the balcony; their new house at Mumbai) Vinaya, this is it – a new beginning, a chance to chase our dreams in the city. Are you ready for this adventure?

Vinaya: Absolutely, Vijay, it's a little bittersweet bidding farewell to our families, but it's time for us to chase our dreams.

Vijay Holding Vinaya's hand, our families have been our support system, and they'll always be a part of our journey. This move is a stepping stone to the life we've envisioned.

Vinaya: True, it's just a temporary farewell. We'll visit them, and they can come to see us. Our dreams are worth the pursuit.

Vijay with determination, we'll make them proud, Vinaya. Our hard work and dedication will speak volumes.

Vinaya: And we'll have each other through it all. That's what matters the most.

Vijay: One year....it just flew in front of our eyes....and now we are here at Mumbai embarking a new journey.

Vinaya: True.... Do you still remember the day we met Varun?

Vijay: How can I forget, Vinaya? It was love at first sight.

Vinaya's words echoed with a touch of nostalgia as she reminisced, "I still vividly remember the day I joined. There you were the epitome of handsomeness on our floor. I tried to resist to look away, but I simply couldn't. It was those enchanting eyes of yours, irresistibly attractive, that held me captivated from the very beginning."

Vijay's gaze lingered on the memory as he shared, "I can still vividly recall the moment you entered the meeting room, adorned in a captivating Pink Salwar. Your silky hair gracefully danced in the air, and that smile of yours—pure radiance, as if it held the sparkle of stars. In that instant, you transformed into a goddess, casting a spell that left me utterly enchanted."

Vinaya: Stop it already, Vijay. Remember the day when you came to propose... the whole floor danced for us. It was an amazing experience.

Vijay: Thanks to my friends, it went well. I was too afraid, thinking whether you would accept my proposal. The moment you said yes, it was like I conquered the whole world.

Vinaya: (leaning on Vijay's shoulders) You are the best thing that happened to my life. I must have done great deeds to get a husband like you.

The bustling city of Mumbai, with its towering skyscrapers and endless opportunities, became the blank canvas for Vijay and Vinaya's dreams. As the evening sun cast a warm glow through the window, Vijay and Vinaya embraced the beauty of the present while eagerly anticipating the unwritten pages of their future as they gracefully embarked on the awaited journey in their lives.

CHAPTER FOUR

TIME'S TICKING

Four years had passed since their enchanting village wedding, and life in the city had engulfed them in a whirlwind of work, ambitions, and the pursuit of financial stability.

Vijay, dedicated to climbing the corporate ladder, poured his energy into his demanding job, while Vinaya, also an IT professional, found herself immersed in the challenging world of technology. Their schedules were relentless, and their focus singular–carves a niche for themselves in the city, earn enough money to lead a comfortable life without any worries.

As they sat in the cozy living room of their home, memories of the past Four years played like a montage in their minds.

Vinaya: Can you believe it's been Four years since we embarked on this adventure?

Vijay smiles, Time flies when we are busy chasing our dreams. Remember when we first came to the city? It feels like a different lifetime.

Vinaya: And now, look at us. We've built a life, faced challenges, and celebrated victories.

Their journey had been a symphony of highs and lows, evidence to their shared resilience and unwavering commitment to each other. From the first promotion to the occasional setbacks, they navigated it all hand in hand.

Vijay: Thank you for being my constant, Vinaya. These Four years have been richer because you're in them.

Vinaya: (leaning on Vijay's shoulders) Likewise, Vijay. Our journey is a story of growth, of evolving together. I wouldn't have it any other way.

The room echoed with the laughter of shared memories, a soundtrack to the chapters of their life. The walls, witness to the triumphs and tribulations, stood as silent storytellers.

The city lights streamed through the window, casting a gentle glow in the living room as Vijay and Vinaya settled into the quiet of their apartment.

The weight of the unspoken had grown over the years, and this evening, it became an undeniable presence in the room.

Vinaya, her gaze fixed on the cityscape outside, took a deep breath. "Vijay," she began her voice a delicate mix of regret and longing, "it's been Four years. Our careers are flourishing, but have you ever thought about the family we dreamed of? We're not getting any younger."

Vijay, feeling the weight of her words, met her eyes with a tinge of guilt. He sighed, the city's buzz outside their window blending with the heavy silence inside. "Vinaya, I know. The city life, the work, it's all been so consuming. But you're right; we can't keep postponing this. We need to find a balance."

Vinaya, her eyes searching his, whispered, "Our dreams are fading into the background. It's like we've put them on hold for so long that they are becoming distant echoes. I don't want to wake up one day and realize that we missed our chance."

Vijay, running his fingers through his hair, nodded in solemn agreement.

"I feel it too, Vinaya. The city has swallowed us whole, and our dreams seem to be slipping away. But what can we do? The demands of our careers, the pace of this city..."

Vinaya, her voice determined, interrupted, "We can't let the city dictate our lives. We moved here for a better future, not to lose sight of what truly matters. Our dreams of a family are as valid as our career aspirations. We owe it to ourselves to try and strike that balance."

Vijay, realizing the truth in her words, took her hands in his. "You're right, Vinaya. We can't let our dreams become casualties of our ambitions. Let's figure this out together. Our love, our dreams, they are worth the effort."

Vinaya: Can you believe our niece Suma is already 5 years old? Varun and Smitha have truly mastered the art of balancing both family and work. I feel like there's so much we can learn from observing how they handle everything.

Vijay nodded in agreement, "Indeed, Vinaya. Balancing family and work is no easy task.

While our parents made their choices; witnessing the dedication and motivation of couples like Varun and Smitha is truly remarkable."

Feeling inspired by Varun and Smitha's ability to manage their responsibilities, the couple decided to take a bold step. They yearned for some quality time with their families and wanted to create memorable experiences before embracing parenthood. With that in mind, they extended heartfelt invitations to both sets of parents and family urging them to visit and share in this special time of their lives. It was a decision filled with anticipation, excitement, and the promise of creating lasting memories.

CHAPTER FIVE

A SYMPHONY OF DREAMS

As the holiday season drew to a close, Vijay and Vinaya found themselves reluctantly parting ways with the laughter and vibrant energy that surrounded their niece, Suma. The joyful moments spent together with their family, during the holidays had created a haven of happiness in their lives.

Vijay looked at Vinaya with a contemplative smile, "You know, love, our home has been so alive with Suma's laughter. It's truly incredible, isn't it?"

Vinaya, her eyes gleaming with a mixture of joy and longing, nodded, "Absolutely, Vijay. This ambiance, filled with happiness, makes me crave the day when we have a little one of our own."

The departure of their family left an emotional void, transforming their once lively home into an empty space where the echoes of laughter were replaced by a somber silence. The absence of loved ones cast a shadow over their hearts, leaving a lingering emptiness that seemed insurmountable.

Vijay, sensing the palpable void, remarked with a bittersweet smile, "Now there's a whole lot of emptiness, Vinaya."

Vinaya, looking into the void, sighed, "It's time to fill that emptiness, Vijay."

And so, the couple embarked on a journey into the intricate world of fertility apps and ovulation calendars. Vijay teased, "Who would have thought our coding skills would be put to the test in such a personal way?"

Vinaya chuckled, "A different kind of coding, indeed. Deciphering the complex patterns of fertility cycles is a challenge of its own."

The decision to start their family infused their lives with a mix of excitement and anticipation. As days turned into weeks and weeks into months, the couple navigated the uncertain journey, eagerly awaiting news that would transform their world.

Vijay, with a glint in his eye, remarked, "Our home will soon echo not just with the sound of coding and technology, but with the laughter of our little one. It's a symphony we are preparing for."

Vinaya, envisioning the future, added, "We'll need to make space for toys, baby clothes, and maybe a rocking chair for those late-night lullabies......."

In the midst of the conversation, Vijay held Vinaya's hand and said, "Our dreams are materializing, love. It's not just about creating a family but also about transforming our home into a heaven were love and laughter reign supreme."

Vinaya leaned forward, her eyes revealing a mixture of excitement and tenderness.

Unable to resist the magnetic pull of Vinaya's presence, Vijay gently cupped her face, his gaze tender yet intense. Vinaya, her eyes reflecting the starlit sky, felt a surge of anticipation coursing through her veins. The air crackled with an undeniable chemistry, a symphony of unspoken emotions swirling around them.

As Vijay leaned in, time seemed to slow. The world around them blurred, leaving only the pulsating energy of that suspended moment. Vinaya closed her eyes, savoring the proximity of Vijay's lips, which lingered tantalizingly close. The scent of his cologne, the warmth of his breath, all merged into a sensory symphony that heightened the anticipation.

Their lips finally met, and it was as if the universe aligned to create a masterpiece in that fleeting second. It wasn't just a kiss; it was a convergence of dreams, a fusion of souls. The softness of their lips against each other was a revelation, igniting a flame that danced between them.

Time resumed its pace, but the magic lingered in the air. When they pulled away, breathless and exhilarated, their eyes met in a silent acknowledgment of the profound connection forged in that kiss. It wasn't just the meeting of lips; it was the initiation of a love story, a promise whispered in the language of hearts.

The balcony, now a witness to their shared intimacy, seemed to breathe with the passion that unfolded. The moon, a silent spectator, bestowed its blessing on the couple, casting a celestial glow over them.

And so, Vijay and Vinaya embraced the profound changes that parenthood would bring, preparing to welcome the harmonious laughter and boundless love of their little one into the symphony of their lives.

CHAPTER SIX

"QUIET STREAMS OF SORROW"

The harmonious melody of lovebirds Vijay and Vinaya found itself drowned out by the relentless whispers of their family members. Every family gathering turned into a stage for well-intentioned inquiries about their family plans, evolving into a relentless chorus that echoed in the corridors of their hearts. Relatives, unknowingly becoming tormentors, relentlessly probed into their personal space, eager to witness the next generation carrying forward the family name.

"Vijay, when will you become a father?"

"Vinaya, you should be holding a little one by now."

The mounting pressure transformed their harmonious life into a discordant symphony. Despite the inner struggles and frustrations, the couple responded with forced smiles, choosing to conceal the challenges they faced. Unbeknownst to them, judgmental gazes were constantly prying, questioning the delay in their journey to parenthood. The unspoken whispers echoed, "Why are they not parents yet?"

At a family gathering, Vijay's aunt, like a maestro directing an unwanted symphony, commented, "Vijay, you've built a successful career, but when will you give us the joy of welcoming a new member into the family?"

Maintaining his composure, Vijay replied, "Auntie, these things take time. We're working on it."

In the quiet corners of their home, the uncomfortable moments unfolded as Vijay and Vinaya faced persistent questions and subtle judgments from relatives. The evening after the family gathering, where prying eyes seemed to linger longer, Vinaya couldn't contain her frustration.

Vinaya sighs, "Vijay, it's getting harder to bear these questions. Every time someone asks, it feels like a tiny piece of our dream is chipped away."

Vijay, pulling her into a comforting embrace: "I know, Vinaya. It's not fair, and I hate seeing you upset. But remember, our journey is unique, and it doesn't need external validations.""Vinaya, I feel the weight too. The expectations, the constant scrutiny, but we can't let it break us. Our love is stronger than their opinions."

Vinaya, wiping away a tear: "I just wish they could understand that this journey is not a race. It's our own, and we'll reach the destination in our time."

Vijay: Vinaya, I am grateful for your unwavering support, felt a renewed strength. You are my better half, and I love you the most.

As every occasion became a battlefield of familial expectations, the couple found strength in their shared vision. Months turned into a year, and the mounting pressure reached its peak. Parents from both ends were worried.

One day Vinaya's mother visited them, unable to hold back her concern, "Vinaya, are you both facing any difficulties? Maybe you should see a doctor."

Vinaya, choosing her words carefully, replied, "Mom, we appreciate your concern, but we're taking it step by step. We'll seek help if needed."

Later that night, as they lay in bed, Vijay reassured her, "Vinaya, our journey is ours alone. Let's not let the noise around us drown out our melody. We'll face this together."

Vinaya: Maybe we should have kept our baby when God gave us a chance earlier.

Vijay: In the dim glow of their bedroom, Vinaya's words lingered in the air like a heavy sigh. Vijay, caressing her hand, responded with gentleness that only love could convey.

Vijay: Vinaya, we made the best decisions we could at the time. We were both scared and uncertain. We can't change the past, but we can shape our future. Our journey to parenthood is still unfolding, and this time, we're more prepared.

Vinaya: I know, Vijay. It's just that sometimes I can't help but wonder how different things would have been if we had chosen differently.

Vijay: We can't dwell on the what-ifs. We are here now, stronger and more committed than ever. Our past decisions don't define us; it's what we do from this moment forward those matters.

Vinaya: (kissing his cheeks) You're right. We have a second chance, and I want us to embrace it with hope and positivity.

Vijay: That's the spirit, Vinaya. We've learned from our past, and now, we move forward together. Our melody is still playing, and it's creating a beautiful symphony of our love and dreams.

As they held onto each other in the quietude of the night, their shared resolve became a beacon of light, cutting through the shadows of the past.

The journey ahead, though uncertain, felt less daunting with the strength of their unity and the promise of a harmonious future. Yet, the sadness lingered, adding a poignant layer to their tale of resilience.

CHAPTER SEVEN

"Shadows of Secrecy: A Secret Past"

The revelation of Vinaya's pregnancy sent seismic tremors into the blank canvas of their nascent dreams, mere months into their wedded bliss. The once-lustrous hues of their shared aspirations dimmed, eclipsed by the looming specter of parenthood. An urgent tension hung thick in the air, demanding an immediate resolution to the unforeseen challenge that had thrown their lives into disarray.

Vinaya: Vijay, we can't let this happen right now. It's too soon for us. We need to discuss.... what to do?

Vijay: Vinaya, let's wait for some time and discuss. Let's talk to Amma and Dada.

Vinaya: There's no time for discussions. We need to act fast. I don't want them to know that I am pregnant. What about our dreams, Vijay?

Vijay anxiously, what should we do now?

The couple, ensnared in the whirlwind of conflicting emotions and practical decisions, found themselves at a critical crossroads. The dreams they had tenderly nurtured together now stood on the precipice of dissolution, challenged by the unexpected arrival of parenthood.

Vijay: Vinaya, I don't want to let go of our dreams, but I can't...

Vinaya: Vijay, our dreams are just taking off. We can't let this disrupt the trajectory we envisioned for our lives.

The urgency of the situation propelled them into a difficult conversation about terminating the pregnancy, a decision that hung heavy on their hearts but seemed inevitable given their circumstances.

Vijay: I hate that it's come to this; we're not ready for parenthood, not now.

The couple, bound by the shared determination to protect their aspirations, embarked on the challenging journey of making an agonizing decision. The emotional turmoil intensified as they grappled with the reality of terminating a life they had not planned for.

As they entered the clinic, heavy silence lingered between them. Vinaya's hand trembled in Vijay's, seeking solace in the midst of an unsettling storm.

Doctor: Vinaya, Vijay, I understand this is a difficult decision. Let's talk about the procedure and any concerns you might have.

Vinaya: We.... we never thought we'd be here, Doctor. It feels like our dreams are slipping away.

Doctor: I know this is tough. Let's discuss the procedure, potential risks, and ensure you have the emotional support you need.

The doctor, a pillar of empathy in the sterile room, guided Vinaya and Vijay through the intricacies of the procedure with utmost sensitivity.

Doctor: The termination procedure involves a series of steps to ensure your well-being. We'll administer medication to induce a miscarriage-like process. It's crucial to understand that the emotional and physical aspects are interconnected during this time.

Vinaya: What about the potential risks, Doctor? Are there complications we should be aware of?

Doctor: Like any medical procedure, there are potential risks, including bleeding, infection, and an incomplete termination.

However, we take every precaution to minimize these risks, and I'll be here to monitor your progress closely.

Vinaya: How long should I stay in the clinic? It's something that we haven't told our parents regarding this pregnancy.

Doctor looks at Vinaya.... Complete silence engulfs the atmosphere for a moment.

Vijay: (anticipating the tension in the surrounding) It's just that we don't want our family to worry.

Doctor: Ok, and she continues.... It's crucial that you take the prescribed medications exactly as instructed. You may experience bleeding, which is a normal part of the process. It's advisable to use sanitary pads rather than tampons to manage the bleeding.

Vinaya: How much bleeding is normal, Doctor?

Doctor: Every woman's experience is different, Vinaya. Some bleeding is expected, similar to a heavy menstrual period. However, if you soak through more than two pads in an hour for two consecutive hours or experience severe pain, it's essential to seek medical attention promptly.

Vijay: We'll make sure to follow your instructions carefully, Doctor.

Doctor: Good. Taking it easy and prioritizing rest is crucial during this time. You might experience cramping, which can be managed with over-the-counter pain relievers, but I'll prescribe something stronger if necessary.

Vinaya: Thank you, Doctor. This is a lot to process, but we appreciate your guidance.

Doctor: I'm here to support you both. Remember, the emotional toll is just as significant as the physical. It's okay to seek counseling or support from friends and family during this time.

Days turned into weeks, and the unspoken grief lingered like a shadow. Each passing moment became a painful reminder of the decision they were forced to make. The shared secret, now heavier than ever, loomed over their relationship like an unyielding storm.

Vinaya: Vijay, I don't know if we have made the right decision. It's still haunting me.

Vijay: It was a combined decision to terminate. Thinking about the past is of no use. Vinaya, sometimes life throws challenges at us that we never anticipated.

The couple grappled with the consequences of their actions, they were prepared to confront the inevitable reckoning that lay ahead—a reckoning not just with their families but with the intricacies of their own hearts and the cost of the secrets they carried.

CHAPTER EIGHT

PRESENT- LOOKING FOR AN EXPERT ADVICE

Vinaya's heart beat with a rhythm of both hope and apprehension, decides to call Smitha, her sister-in-law, seeking guidance on the daunting journey into parenthood. In the hushed intimacy of the moment, she dared to mention the delicate subject that lingered in the air like unspoken fate.

Vinaya (over the phone): "Smitha," if you are free at the moment, can I speak with you for ten minutes. Vinaya began, her voice a mixture of vulnerability and determination, "as my sister and a doctor, your advice is invaluable. We're standing at the precipice of parenthood. If the natural path proves elusive, what options do we have?"

Smitha, caught between the roles of a medical professional and a caring sister, hesitated momentarily before delivering a truth that carried the weight of both worlds. "There are options like IUI and IVF," she began, her words hanging in the air like a delicate confession. "Professionally, I'd recommend them, but, honestly, as your sister, I must say it's a big no from me. Fertility procedures, especially IVF, come with a myriad of complications."

As the gravity of IVF unfolded, Smitha painted a vivid picture of the intricate process, the challenges, and the potential pitfalls that awaited. Vinaya, absorbing the technicalities, furrowed her brow, seeking to grasp the full scope.

"What kind of complications are we talking about?" she asked, her voice a whisper carrying the weight of impending decisions.

Smitha, carefully choosing her words, delved into the physical and emotional toll. "Physically, the fertility drugs used for ovarian stimulation can lead to discomfort, and in some cases, complications like ovarian hyper stimulation syndrome. The egg retrieval process carries risks of infection or bleeding. Emotionally, the journey is draining, with the highs and lows of hope, and the financial strain taking a toll on individuals and relationships."

Vinaya, grappling with the newfound knowledge, whispered in contemplation, "So, even if we endure all of this, there's no guarantee it will work?"

Smitha nodded empathetically, her eyes reflecting shared understanding. "Exactly. Success rates vary, and it can be emotionally challenging if things don't go as planned. That's why, as your sister, I lean towards exploring alternatives that are gentler on both body and mind."

Intrigued by the prospect of a more natural path, Vinaya inquired further, "Do you know anyone here in Mumbai who practices Ayurveda?"

Smitha, in the dual role of sister and advisor, took a moment to contemplate. "Hmmm, I need to check. I remember reading about a renowned practitioner named Dr. Samarth who runs an Ayurveda clinic at Mumbai. I'll share the details with you. It might be worth consulting him."

Smitha spoke words that resonated with a blend of familial warmth and medical wisdom. "Vinaya, I understand the dream, and I share it with you. My suggestion, considering both roles I wear, would be to explore Ayurveda. It's a more holistic approach, aligning with our roots. There's a balance in natural methods that resonates well with many."

As the novel unfolded, this chapter became a turning point, marked by serious discussions, shared dreams, and the realization that the journey to parenthood wasn't a straightforward path but a complex exploration of choices, traditions, and personal beliefs.

The narrative delved deeper into the intricate dance between modern medicine and ancient wisdom, paving the way for a story that would unfold with unexpected twists and poignant moments.

CHAPTER NINE

WHISPERS OF HOPE

As the days slipped through their fingers like grains of sand, the whispers of hope became an unrelenting hum, each month's unmet expectation etching a shadow on the canvas of their dreams.

Vinaya and Vijay, locked in their silent struggle, explored natural conception methods of Ayurveda, suggested by Smitha, hoping to find a gentler path to parenthood.

The herbal fragrances of Ayurvedic remedies gave the couple a new hope to embrace. Vinaya's eyes mirrored the dance of emotions in her heart, and Vijay, holding her hand, felt a renewed sense of expectation, ready to face whatever lay ahead.

As the discussion unfolded, Vinaya and Vijay bared their souls, sharing the intricate details of their journey, their previous attempts, and their medical experiences. Dr. Samarth listened attentively, providing expert insights and outlining the tailored plan for their natural conception journey through Ayurveda.

Vinaya: Dr. Samarth, what are the success rates, and what can we expect emotionally and physically?

Dr. Samarth: Success rates vary, and each case is unique. Physically, there will be lifestyle adjustments and Ayurvedic treatments. Emotionally, it's crucial to provide each other with unwavering support. The journey can be challenging, but many couples find success and fulfillment through Ayurvedic methods.

Vijay: We're ready for this, Dr. Samarth. Our dream of having a family is paramount to us.

Dr. Samarth: That's the spirit. Communication and emotional support are key throughout the process. We'll tailor a plan that suits your specific situation.

Exiting the doctor's office, Vijay and Vinaya engaged in a heartfelt conversation.

Vinaya: This is a journey, Vijay. We're in it together, no matter what.

Vijay: Absolutely, Vinaya. Our love is the foundation, and together, we'll navigate this path.

Fortified with information and a shared resolve, they stepped into the world of natural conception through Ayurveda. The whispers of society were momentarily silenced as they embarked on this deeply personal journey, echoing with the hope that their dreams of parenthood would soon be realized.

Days turned into a patient waiting game, and the looming financial concerns cast shadows on their hopes. The expenditure seemed insurmountable, but the determination to become parents burned brighter than the challenges they faced.

Balancing financial prudence with the persistent ache for parenthood, they found a flicker of hope. They embraced the journey of Ayurvedic methods, knowing it would be demanding, yet holding onto the belief that it could unlock the door to their dreams.

Then, in a twist of fate, after a long and patient wait, they had naturally conceived through Ayurveda.

The joy was overwhelming, and after confirming the news through home pregnancy test, they found themselves once again in the comforting presence of Dr. Samarth.

Dr. Samarth: Congratulations! The Ayurvedic treatments and lifestyle adjustments would have enhanced the fertility.

Vinaya: Dr. Samarth. What should we do now?

Dr. Samarth: Let's proceed with the necessary tests and monitoring to ensure a healthy and smooth pregnancy. Nature has its way of surprising us, and I'm here to guide you through this new chapter.

Vinaya: Vijay, we're going to be parents. Can you believe it?

Vijay: Vinaya, this journey has been unpredictable, but look at the miracle we're about to witness. Our love has prevailed through every storm.

As the chapter unfolded, the couple realized that sometimes, the most beautiful stories are written by the hand of fate. In the gentle cradle of Dr. Samarth's expertise and their enduring love, Vinaya and Vijay prepared to welcome the unexpected yet cherished chapter of parenthood with open hearts and tearful gratitude.

CHAPTER TEN

THE DANCE OF CREATION

In a small, hygienic room, the air was charged with the sweet scent of anticipation, and dreams hung in the balance, ready to be woven into reality. Vinaya laid on the examination table, her eyes locked with Vijay's, a silent exchange of hope and excitement passing between them, a beautiful painting of their shared journey.

The couple, hearts entwined, eagerly awaited their first ultrasound scan. Clasping each other's hands, they brimmed with enthusiasm, knowing that the path ahead was shrouded in uncertainties. Breathless, they awaited the moment when the ultrasound would unveil the heartbeat, the tangible proof of their dreams taking form within Vinaya's womb.

Under the guidance received from Dr. Samarth, the couple decided to visit a diagnostic center for the ultrasound scan. The room, bathed in dim light and humming with the rhythm of medical instruments, became a sacred space for their hopes and fears. As the ultrasound wand glided gently over Vinaya's belly, time stood still.

The radiologist, a weaver of stories yet untold, held the power to reveal the next chapter in this extraordinary tale.

Vinaya, her voice soft with emotion, whispered to Vijay, "Can you believe we've come this far?"

His eyes filled with warmth and love, he asked, "Are you okay, love?"

Vinaya nodded, "I'm more than okay. We've created a life together, Vijay. It's surreal, isn't it?"

Vijay squeezed her hand, a reassuring smile on his face, "We've been through so much together, Vinaya. This is just another step in our journey. Whatever happens, we face it together."

As the radiologist examined the ultrasound images, the couple's hearts beat in sync with the ticking clock.

Then came the revelation, unexpected and profound: "Congratulations. It seems there's a single embryo inside the uterus."

A stunned silence filled the room, broken only by the exchanged glances of the couple. "Wow, a baby?" they echoed in disbelief.

The radiologist, with a smile, affirmed, "Yes, indeed. You're expecting. I can see a gestational sac. You are 4 weeks pregnant, Vinaya."

Vinaya's eyes widened in astonishment, "Vijay, did you hear that?"

Vijay, his voice filled with a mix of shock and awe, responded, "Are you serious? We are going to be parents."

The radiologist, with a reassuring smile, nodded, "Absolutely. The room pulsated with the weight of the revelation.

Vinaya, still processing the news, turned to Vijay, "I can't believe it. Our family is about to get even more beautiful.

" Vijay, still in disbelief, chuckled nervously, "A baby! That's... that's amazing.

Vinaya squeezed his hand, a mixture of excitement and trepidation in her eyes, This is a miracle, and we're in this journey together, no matter what.

" Vijay, looking at the ultrasound images on the screen, whispered, "The joy, the responsibility. But hey, we're in for the ride of our lives."

As they exchanged glances, the reality of their impending parenthood sank in.

The radiologist, observing their emotional exchange, said, "It's a delightful surprise, isn't it? He added "But patience is the key. In two weeks, we'll get a clearer picture of the development and confirm the heartbeat."

As reality sank in, the room echoed with a mix of shock, joy, and the realization that their lives were about to take an unexpected turn.

The radiologist, observing the couple's reactions, reassured them, "Take your time to absorb the news. Congratulations again, and I'll see you in two weeks for the follow-up.

"The chapter continued to unfold, promising new beginnings and the magic of a dream fulfilled, with the couple realizing that their journey to parenthood had just become even more extraordinary".

CHAPTER ELEVEN

DREAMS AT LOSE

Two long weeks had passed since Vinaya eagerly awaited her ultrasound scan. Now, lying on the sterile examination bed, she tightly held her husband's hand, her gaze fixed on the ultrasound screen. The air was thick with a blend of heart-wrenching sadness and anxiety as the technician glided the ultrasound wand over Vinaya's belly.

Vinaya: Where is the radiologist whom we previously met?

Technician: He is busy at the moment. I will send a word, if you want to meet him; let's focus on the scan Ma'am.

The screen, instead of revealing the promise of life, showcased an image that shattered their dreams.

Technician: I'm sorry.

Couple: (Faces falling, exchanging worried glances).

Couple: What happened?

Technician: (Taking a deep breath) I couldn't detect any heartbeat. I'm truly sorry.

Couple: Are you sure? Could there be a mistake?

Technician: I understand this is incredibly difficult to hear. I'll double-check my findings, but it appears that there's no development.

Silence enveloped the room, a heavy, suffocating silence, broken only by the distant hum of medical equipment. The couple, grappling with the abrupt shift from excitement to devastation, clung to a flicker of hope that there might be an error.

Couple: What!... what do we do now?

Technician: I'll consult with the doctor, and we'll discuss the next steps. It's important to take some time to process this information.

The couple, their initial joy replaced by heart-wrenching sorrow, now faced the painful reality of loss. The technician, her expression reflecting empathy, prepared to leave the room.

Vinaya, her voice choked with sadness, pleaded, "Can we talk to the radiologist? Is it possible for him to come and check again?"

Technician: Sure, ma'am.

Radiologist: (Entering the room with a sympathetic demeanor) I heard about the difficult news. I'm truly sorry for what you're going through.

Couple: (Eyes filled with tears) Can there be any mistake, doctor?

Radiologist: I understand how challenging this is. The technician has reviewed the findings, and unfortunately, there is no growth. I wish the outcome was different.

Couple: What do we do now?

Radiologist: I'll consult with the medical team, and we'll discuss the options moving forward. It's crucial to take the time, as you both need to process this.

The room became heavy with sorrow as the couple absorbed the devastating reality. The radiologist, acknowledging the weight of the moment, stepped out to confer with the medical team about the couple's next steps. In the midst of their shattered joy, the couple now faced the painful journey of navigating loss and making decisions about what comes next.

Devastation gripped Vinaya's heart as reality sank in—their single miracle is not growing; their dreams are shattered. The once palpable joy had evaporated, leaving behind an ache that seemed insurmountable. In that moment of heartbreak, Vinaya found strength in her decision to make a bold, painful choice. With tear-stained eyes and a heavy heart, she faced the unfathomable truth—she needed to let go.

The subsequent days melted into a blur of hospitalizations, tear-stained pillows, and silent grief. Vinaya, once a beacon of life and hope, now bore the burden of loss within her.

The once vibrant room now witnessed the courage of a woman who, in the face of unbearable loss, chose to take control of her shattered dreams. The decision to terminate was not an easy one.

As Vinaya embarked on the painful journey of saying goodbye to her single miracle, she clung to the fragments of hope that remained. In the days that followed the heartbreaking news, Vijay and Vinaya found solace in each other's presence. Their conversations were tender, filled with shared sorrow and the struggle to come to terms with their shattered dreams.

Vijay gently held Vinaya's hand, his eyes reflecting the pain in hers. "Vinaya, I can't imagine what you're going through. But we're in this together, every step of the way."

Vinaya nodded, her voice barely above a whisper, "Vijay, it's like a part of us is gone. The dreams we had for our baby... it feels like they were snatched away."

Vijay pulled her into an embrace, "I know, love. Our hearts ache together. But we have each other, and we'll find a way through this darkness."

As the days progressed, Vinaya began coming out of her shell. She managed a faint smile, "We're a team, Vijay. I couldn't do this without you by my side." There is still hope for us.

Will they survive the turmoil? Do they still hold hopes to embark parenthood? The upcoming chapters disclose the purity in their relationship and the vast experiences that lie ahead of them.

CHAPTER TWELVE

THE GARDEN OF HOPE

The Garden of Hope had long been shrouded in the dense fog of uncertainty that clung to Vinaya and Vijay's lives. Two years of winding through the labyrinth of despair had etched lines of resilience on their faces. Yet, they clung to each other, their love a steadfast anchor in the tumultuous sea of their journey.

One fateful day, a subtle breeze of change whispered through the air, catching Vinaya's attention. Two missed periods – the heralds of a possibility, the faint echo of life within her. An anxious tremor gripped her as she grappled with the thought of a long-awaited pregnancy.

"Vijay, something is amiss," she confessed, her voice tinged with uncertainty. "I need to take a test. What if I am pregnant? What if the weight of motherhood becomes too much for us to bear?"

Vijay, the unwavering pillar of support, squeezed her hand, his eyes reflecting both concern and determination.

"Vinaya, doubt is a natural companion on this journey. But we're ready for whatever destiny has in store. Our love has weathered storms; this, too, shall be a chapter in our tale."

As Vinaya's nervous fingers clutched the positive pregnancy test, a cocktail of emotions stirred within her. Joy collided with fear, and the shadows of past heartbreaks loomed large. Seeking solace and guidance, they turned to Smitha, their confidante and sister-in-law. The conversation unfolded over the phone.

Vinaya: (Over the phone) Hi Smitha, I wanted to talk to you; It's a bit important.

Smitha: What happened Vinaya? Tell me.

Vinaya: It's been two months since I missed my periods. I did the test in the morning, and yes, it's positive. Vijay and I are overjoyed, but given our history, I'm also anxious.

Smitha: First of all, congratulations! I understand your concerns, though.

We should get you to a gynecologist for a check-up. It's essential to monitor your health closely, especially considering your past experiences.

Vinaya: That's exactly what we were thinking. We want to ensure everything is okay.

Smitha: It's a positive sign, but it's wise to be cautious. Let's schedule a visit to the doctor. They'll be able to provide the necessary guidance and ensure you have the right support throughout this journey. I have a friend who has a clinic at Mumbai, it would be wise to visit her. Her name is Priya; I will share her phone number.

Vinaya: Thank you, Smitha. Your support means a lot.

Smitha: We'll take this one step at a time. I'll help you schedule the appointment with Priya, and we'll ensure everything is in place for a healthy pregnancy.I will also give you the number of the radiologist; his name is Pream. He works in Priya's clinic.

In this telephone exchange, Smitha's support spans the distance, bridging the gap with empathy and immediate suggestions for proactive steps to address concerns and prioritize the health of both Vinaya and the developing pregnancy.

As the days stretched the hope manifested itself like a delicate sprout pushing through the cracks of despair. The journey, laden with heartache, had led them to this moment—the promise of life growing within Vinaya's womb.

The days progressed, and the garden of hope, once fraught with thorns, now yielded the delicate blossoms of promise. Hand in hand, Vinaya and Vijay emerged from the shadows, ready to script the next chapter of their lives – a chapter that held the promise of a new beginning, where the echoes of their shared journey resonated in the laughter of a new life.

CHAPTER THIRTEEN

DOUBLE MIRACLE THE RELEVATION- PART 1

Undeterred by the twists and turns of their journey, Vinaya and Vijay decided to embark on a new chapter. The enthusiasm and persistence in their quest for parenthood had reached a crescendo, setting the stage for a revelation.

In the weeks that followed, hope and apprehension intertwined, creating a symphony of emotions. The rhythmic beat of a heartbeat became the anthem of their journey towards parenthood. As they entered the ultrasound room, anticipation hung thick in the air. Pream, the radiologist, greeted them with a warm smile.

Ultrasound Room: Pream: Hi Vinaya, Smitha called me and informed me regarding the Scan. How are you feeling today?

Vinaya: Nervous, excited, a bit of everything.

Pream: Well, let's take a look and see how things are progressing. Lie back comfortably, Vinaya.

Vinaya: Okay, here goes nothing.

Pream: (During the ultrasound) There it is. That tiny flicker you see on the screen – that's your baby's heartbeat. Can you hear the sound?

Vinaya: Oh my, really? It's... it's amazing.

Pream: Everything looks good. A strong heartbeat is a positive sign. Congratulations, Vinaya.

Vinaya: Thank you, Doctor Pream. Thank you so much.

In the hushed atmosphere of Dr. Pream's office, the words confirming the health of the growing embryos were delivered with a precision that hung in the air. The room seemed to hold its breath as Pream, with a knowing smile, added an unexpected twist to the narrative.

Pream: Another surprising element I would like to add here.

Vinaya: (leaning in) What is that?

Pream: (with a twinkle in the eye) There is not just one but two perfectly growing embryos inside you.

A pause enveloped the room as Vinaya's eyes widened in astonishment.

Vinaya (whispering): Incredible! I'm going to become a mother of twins... it's truly amazing. Thank you, dear God.

The revelation echoed like a sweet melody, resonating through the corners of their hearts. The journey through pregnancy transformed into a delicate dance, every movement a step in the choreography of protecting the burgeoning lives within. Vinaya, now navigating the delicate balance of carrying precious cargo, embraced a new set of guidelines.

Pream: No heavy lifting, a diet rich in nutrients, a stress-free work environment – providing the optimal conditions for the double miracle growing within you.

As Vinaya returned home, the air was charged with an unspoken excitement. Vijay, eager to hear about the checkup, was met with Vinaya's beaming smile.

Vijay: How was the checkup, love?

Vinaya: Vijay, you won't believe it. I heard the heartbeat today. We are going to be parents.... Yay! But that's not all.

Vijay: What is it?

Vinaya handed him the ultrasound image, anticipation written all over her face.

Vinaya: Look at the scan image... can you see two circles there... it's a double miracle, Vijay. Can you believe it?

The room seemed to shimmer with an invisible magic as the reality of expecting twins sunk in. Vijay, caught in a whirlwind of emotions, gazed at the ultrasound image, realizing that their journey had just taken an exhilarating and unexpected turn. The atmosphere buzzed with the enchantment of the double miracle that awaited them.

Vinaya: The doctor said everything looks good. I am going to treasure these little ones.

Vijay: I knew it. Our journey is turning into something beautiful.

Vinaya: Vijay, the doctor gave me a list of things to follow during the pregnancy – no heavy lifting, a balanced diet, and a stress-free environment.

Vijay: Hmm.... Yeah, we'll make sure everything is perfect for you and the babies. I can handle the heavy lifting around the house.

Vinaya: And I need you to remind me to take those prenatal vitamins daily. Doctor's orders....

Vijay: Consider it done. It's time that we share the news with our family officially.

Vinaya: Vijay, let's call our parents and share the news. I want them to be a part of this journey.....

(Continued....)

Double Miracle- Part 2

The excitement in Vijay and Vinaya's hearts was too contagious to be contained, and they couldn't wait to share the news of expecting twins with their parents. With bated breaths and joy brimming in their voices, they decided to make the calls that would spread the enchanting news.

With smiles on their faces, Vijay and Vinaya dialed the phone. "Are you ready, Vinaya?" asked Vijay.

Vinaya: Absolutely, Vijay. This is going to be the best news ever.

Vijay: Absolutely, Vinaya. They'll be over the moon.

Vinaya: (On the phone) Mom, Dad, guess what? I am pregnant, and we heard the heartbeat today! We are expecting double miracle.

Parents: (Excited voices on the phone) Oh, that's wonderful news!

Vijay: Vinaya, look at you. You're glowing.

Vinaya: It's the happiness, Vijay. I never thought we'd come this far.

Vijay: (On the phone) Dada and Amma, guess what? We are going to be parents. Its twins.

Upon hearing Vijay's words, Sidharth and Manju were filled with boundless joy! Amidst the buzzing excitement in the household, little did they realize that Suma, now a keen 7-year-old observer, was eavesdropping on this exhilarating revelation.

Suma, unable to contain her excitement, snatched the phone and spoke; eyes radiant with curiosity. "Aunty Vinaya, I'm so happy! Twins in your tummy! Wow, I can't wait to meet the little ones."

Vinaya, caught off guard but delighted by Suma's enthusiasm, smiled warmly, "Thank you, Suma! We're over the moon, and you'll be the best big sister ever."

Uncle Vijay, chiming in, affirmed, "Absolutely, Suma! This is a special time for our family, and you'll have little babies to play with and take care of."

Their conversations echoed the joy and anticipation that surrounded the twins growing within Vinaya. Each moment became a shared celebration, strengthening the bond between them and laying the foundation for the wonders yet to come.

Vijay, overwhelmed with joy and love, held Vinaya close, their hearts beating in synchrony. In a moment charged with emotion, he leaned in and pressed his lips against hers in an intense and passionate kiss. The world around them seemed to fade as the connection between them deepened, sealing their shared happiness and the promise of a beautiful journey ahead. As they lingered in the embrace of that fervent kiss, time stood still, encapsulating the sheer magic of the twins that had ignited their lives.

Vijay: Our twins. I can't wait to meet our little ones.

Vinaya: (Resting her hand on her belly) Me neither. This journey, with all its challenges, is the most beautiful thing we've ever done.

As the days went by, the twins blossomed into a tangible reality. Vinaya's belly swelled with the lives that had once been a mere flicker on the ultrasound screen. The couple, now enveloped in the warmth of impending parenthood, marveled at the journey they had undertaken.

The chapter unfolded with grace and wonder, a testament to the resilience of love and the unwavering faith that fueled their journey. Amidst the complexities faced by the couple, Vinaya and Vijay found solace in the simplicity of two heartbeats, two lives that embodied the essence of their dreams.

The news of Vinaya's pregnancy and the enchanting heartbeats had rippled through their families like a wave of joy. Determined to share in the anticipation and offer unwavering support, the entire family decides to visit Mumbai.

The story, far from reaching its conclusion, continued to paint the intricate canvas of landscape with new beginnings and the magic of twins.

CHAPTER FOURTEEN

WHISPERS OF WORRY

The air in the room hung heavy with anticipation as Vinaya, in the first trimester of her pregnancy, found herself facing unexpected challenges. The initial joy of expecting twins had now given way to a moment of concern, as she experienced cramping and noticed mild bleeding. Anxiety etched across her face, Vinaya hesitated but realized the gravity of the situation. It was time to seek guidance and reassurance from Priya, her trusted gynecologist.

Vinaya: (whispering to herself) It's probably nothing, just a little discomfort. (Feeling a cramp) But I need to make sure everything is okay.

With a furrowed brow, she approached Priya's clinic, the walls seemingly holding the answers to her worries. Smitha, her ever-watchful sister, noticed the subtle change in Vinaya's demeanor and decided to accompany her for support.

Inside Priya's clinic, the atmosphere was a blend of sterile calmness and the delicate scent of antiseptic. The receptionist greeted them with a warm smile, unaware of the turbulence within Vinaya's heart. As they sat in the waiting area, Smitha offered a reassuring smile.

Finally, the moment arrived as Priya's assistant requested Vinaya into the consultation room. Priya, a figure of serene confidence, welcomed her patient with a warm smile.

Priya: Vinaya, how are you feeling today?

Vinaya: Priya, I've been having cramps and noticed some bleeding. I'm so worried about the babies.

Priya, with a calm and assuring demeanor, guided Vinaya to lie on the examination table. The room seemed to hold its breath as Priya conducted the necessary examinations.

Priya: (examining Vinaya) Let's take a look and see what's going on. Try to stay calm.

With each passing second, the tension in the room became palpable. Smitha, waiting outside, appeared anxious, eager to discover the reason behind Vinaya's sudden meeting with Priya.

Priya: (after the examination, smiling) Vinaya, the babies are doing well. The cramping and bleeding might be due to various reasons, but it doesn't seem to pose an immediate threat.

Vinaya, overwhelmed with relief, felt tears welling up in her eyes.

Vinaya: Thank you, Priya. I was so scared.

Priya: It's normal to feel anxious, especially with twins. But we'll monitor the situation closely. Remember, I'm here to support you throughout this journey.

As Vinaya left Priya's clinic, still carrying the weight of the recent scare, Smitha noticed her subdued demeanor. Sensing something amiss, Smitha approached Vinaya with concern etched across her face.

Smitha: (placing a gentle hand on Vinaya's shoulder) Vinaya, what happened in there? You seem to be in discomfort.

Vinaya: Oh, it's probably nothing, just a little scare. Priya said everything should be fine.

Smitha: Vinaya, don't brush it off. Tell me what's going on. I can see it in your eyes.

Vinaya hesitated, torn between her desire to share and the fear of burdening Smitha with her worries.

Vinaya: Okay, Smitha, I did experience some cramping and noticed mild bleeding. But Priya assured me it might not be a big issue.

Smitha: Vinaya, why didn't you tell me earlier? I am also a doctor. You can't keep something like this to yourself.

Vinaya: I didn't want to worry you or anyone in the family, Smitha. Priya said it might be common, and I didn't want to make a big deal out of it.

Smitha: Vinaya, our family bond goes beyond worrying. We're in this together. Now, tell me, is there anything else I need to know?

Vinaya, touched by Smitha's genuine concern, took a deep breath and shared more details about her recent experience. Smitha listened attentively, offering words of comfort and reassurance.

Smitha: Vinaya, we're navigating this journey together the whole family is here for your support. If you ever feel scared or uncertain, promise me you'll share it with me. We're sisters, and I want to be there for you, no matter what.

Their connection, already a sturdy bond, became an even more crucial anchor during this challenging time. As they walked away from Priya's clinic, Smitha, determined to be a pillar of strength, embraced Vinaya in a warm and reassuring hug.

The resonances of their shared conversation lingered, adding another layer of shades to the intricate, colorful canvas of their sisterhood.

CHAPTER FIFTEEN

6TH MONTH PREGNANCY

The sixth month of Vinaya's pregnancy unfolded with an ominous intensity, akin to a turbulent storm casting shadows over their once bright horizon of anticipation. Her body, once a sanctuary of burgeoning life, now bore the weight of swelling that defied the boundaries of normalcy, an unwelcome intrusion into the blissful journey they had envisioned.

Vinaya, resilient and determined, clung desperately to the flicker of hope that had initially ignited their joyous journey. The babies, once a beacon of shared dreams, now became a source of strength amid the encroaching uncertainty that clouded their once joyful days. The couple, their hearts entwined with the promise of impending parenthood, refused to relinquish their grip on hope, even as shadows deepened around them.

Suddenly, an alarming turn of events shattered the fragile tranquility. Overwhelmed by the strain on her body, Vinaya collapsed, her entire form swollen and fragile. Panic surged through the room, a palpable force, as concerned family members rushed to her side.

Vijay, his voice laced with urgency and fear, shouted, "Vinaya! Vinaya! Someone call for help!

Smitha, her face etched with worry and determination, commanded, "Get the car immediately! We have to get her to the clinic right away!"

In the urgency of the moment, the once calm and controlled atmosphere crumbled, giving way to a whirlwind of anxiety. The air crackled with tension as they swiftly moved Vinaya into the car, the vehicle becoming a lifeline in a storm of uncertainty.

Hurried footsteps echoed through the clinic's corridors as the once-distant hum of medical equipment loomed closer. The family, faces etched with worry, gathered around Vinaya as the medical team rushed to assess the dire situation.

Priya, "What happened?"

Vijay, his voice strained with worry, responded, "She fainted, and her body is so swollen. We don't know what's happening."

Priya, devoid of reassurance, declared, "Prep her for immediate examination. We need to find out what's causing this."

Vinaya's limp form was transferred to an examination bed. The clinic, once a routine stop in the journey of pregnancy, now transformed into a battleground where the fight for both Vinaya's and the babies' well-being intensified.

The air thickened with tension as Priya's medical team conducted tests and examinations. Vijay, standing on the sidelines, could hardly bear the weight of uncertainty that hung in the room. The once hopeful journey had taken an unexpected and treacherous turn, plunging them into a maelstrom of fear and confusion.

Priya, the gravity of the situation evident in her words, declared, "We need to stabilize her immediately. The swelling and fainting are signs of a critical condition. We'll have to monitor her closely."

The news hit the family like a sledgehammer, the reality of the situation sinking in. The clinic, once a place of routine check-ups and joyous scans, now bore witness to a stark reality—a battle against an unseen adversary that threatened the very core of Vinaya's pregnancy.

In the clinic's sterile environment, amidst the beeping machines and antiseptic scent, Vinaya clung to the tiny life within her, a fragile beacon in the storm of uncertainty.

Priya, with a mix of concern and helplessness etched on her face, confided in Smitha, "We're dealing with a critical situation here. If we don't handle the signs and symptoms meticulously with the right care and medication, there's a significant risk of preterm birth. Considering potential issues there could be breathing and feeding difficulties, vision or hearing problems, developmental delays...

Smitha: What should I tell the family? They are all extremely worried.

Priya: I can address the situation with medications, but I can't predict how long it'll be effective. Vinaya is in a weakened state and requires round-the-clock monitoring. Convey to the family that it's imperative for her to be here; otherwise, there is a significant risk of miscarriage given her current condition."

Surrounded by love and empathy, the family grappled with the gravity of the news, wrapping Vinaya in their collective concern.

Varun: Everyone, we've received the doctor's update. The situation is dire.

Vinaya's Father: This is unbearable. How did we reach this point?

Vinaya's Mother: My daughter... What about the babies? Will they be okay?

Varun: Is there anything we can do to ensure their wellbeing? This feels like a nightmare.

The hospital room turned into a stage, bearing witness to the resilience of a couple who had dared to dream, only to confront the harsh reality of impending news about a potential miscarriage, shattering their aspirations.

As the tension in the hospital room peaked, Vijay stood in a corner, utterly bewildered and at a loss for words. The gravity of the situation weighed heavily on him, rendering him speechless. The enormity of the news they heard left him immobilized, his mind swirling with a tumult of emotions from despair to disbelief. Amidst such intense distress, Vijay found himself incapable of contributing to the discussions or providing the support he so desperately longed to offer.

Tears filled Vinaya's eyes as she confronted the harsh reality that she might lose the little ones growing within her if the situation worsened.

Priya: Please don't cry, Vinaya. I'm committed to doing everything within my power for both of you. We'll closely monitor the babies using Doppler, and if necessary, I can adjust the medication dosage. Currently, you are in your 24th week of pregnancy, and our objective is to extend it up to 28 weeks for a safe pre-term delivery. Throughout this period, you must stay in my clinic; here we've arranged designated rooms for you. Our devoted nursing staff will provide round-the-clock monitoring. Rest assured, I am dedicated to ensuring the well-being of both you and the babies.

The chapter, marked by echoes of heartache, unfolded with a poignant acknowledgment of the fragility of life. Amidst the pain and grief, the family clung to each other, their shared sorrow a testament to the profound love that had bound them together on this tumultuous journey.

The room, once a stage for an inevitable ending, now bore witness to the fervent desire to defy fate and grasp onto a thread of hope, no matter how fragile.

CHAPTER SIXTEEN

"The Threads of Choices"

The journey Vijay and Vinaya had embarked upon with dreams of parenthood now seemed like an insurmountable mountain, casting shadows over the love that once flourished. Vijay, once the pillar of support, found himself drowning in frustration. The emotional toll of dashed hopes became an unbearable burden. His dreams of a happy family started to morph into a nightmare, and in the midst of his anguish, he began directing his frustration towards Vinaya.

Vinaya, equally shattered by the repeated disappointments, felt the sharp edge of Vijay's growing resentment. The joy they once shared was replaced by heated arguments and accusatory glances. The struggles that were meant to bring them closer had become a wedge driving them apart.

Vijay: Vinaya, all these complications with the pregnancy are because of your past decisions! You should have never done that abortion.

Vinaya: Vijay, it's not fair to blame me for everything. We made that decision together.

Vijay: All you wanted was to chase your dreams. You were so irresponsible. See, we are facing all these because of you.

Vinaya: Don't turn this into a blame game, Vijay. We both agreed to our choices back then.

Vijay: Your dreams always came first. Maybe if we had prioritized having a family....You are the one to be blamed.

Vinaya: I can't believe you're saying this. We faced challenges together, and now you're blaming me?

Vijay: Maybe..... Maybe if you had been little more careful, things would be different. Why do you put your career first?

Vinaya: My career is not the problem here! We both made choices, and now we have to deal with the consequences together.

Vijay: I just feel like we've made so many mistakes, and now it's affecting our chance at having a healthy family.

Vinaya: It's....... It's not just about the past, Vijay. It's about how we handle things now. We can't change what happened, but we can support each other through this.

In this heated conversation, emotions run high as Vijay vents his frustrations and places blame on past decisions. Vinaya, feeling unfairly accused, defends their shared choices and emphasizes the importance of facing the present challenges together. Vinaya, now confined to a hospital bed, grappled with the uncertainty surrounding her babies' well-being, while Vijay, fueled by frustration, unleashed his anger in a storm of accusations.

Vijay: Vinaya, do you realize the financial mess we're in because of all these hospital charges? It's like everything is falling apart, and you just stand there, clueless.

Vinaya: Vijay, it's not like I asked for these complications. We're both in this together, and the financial strain is as much my concern as it is yours.

Vijay: If we didn't have to deal with all these issues, we wouldn't be drowning in medical bills. Your decisions, our past mistakes – they're all catching up to us.

Vinaya: Are you aware of the pain I've been undergoing since the beginning of the pregnancy? Have I told any of that to you? No, right? Please, Vijay, calm down. I'm enduring all of this for our babies. I'm not in a state for such silly, nonsensical fights.

Late-night discussions were no longer filled with laughter that once echoed in their home now seemed like a distant memory. The love that was once their strength became a source of pain, each unfulfilled longing tearing at the fabric of their connection.

The chapter unfolds with the couple at a crossroads, the echoes of their struggles resonating in the once-happy home. As they navigate the storm of anger and resentment, the question looms: Can their love withstand the trials of parenthood, or will the bitterness consume the foundation they built together?

CHAPTER SEVENTEEN

THE GUIDING LIGHT

In the midst of the storm of anger and resentment between Vijay and Vinaya, the room in the clinic now resembled a battleground. The echoes of their heated arguments reached the ears of Smitha, who, by chance, overheard the turmoil as she entered the room to check on Vinaya. Concern etched on her face; she entered the scene like a soothing breeze in the midst of a tempest.

Smitha: What's going on here?

Vijay and Vinaya, caught off guard by Smitha's unexpected presence, exchanged uneasy glances.

Vinaya: It's nothing, Smitha. Just a disagreement.

Smitha: Disagreements don't usually involve slamming doors and raised voices. Now, what's really going on?

Vijay, struggling with his emotions, finally spoke up.

Vijay: We're just frustrated, Smitha. This journey to become parents is tearing us apart.

Smitha: I understand it's challenging, but fighting won't make it any easier. You both need patience and understanding right now. Don't forget that there's a life growing inside Vinaya.

The weight of Smitha's words hung in the air, a poignant reminder that amidst their strife, a tiny heartbeat persisted.

Vinaya: It's just so hard, Smitha. We never imagined it would be like this.

Smitha: I know, my dear. But now is not the time to let frustration tear you apart. You need each other more than ever. This journey requires unity, not division.

Smitha's wisdom and unwavering support began to quell the storm within Vijay and Vinaya. The realization that they still carried the hope of new lives within them became a grounding force.

Smitha: Take a deep breath, both of you. Patience is your ally in this struggle. The love that brought you together can also see you through this challenging chapter. Lean on each other, and remember, family sticks together in the face of adversity. Leave everything in the past and live in the present.

Vinaya: Thank you, Smitha. We need to focus on what truly matters.

As Smitha engaged in conversation with Vinaya and Vinaya, the atmosphere took an unexpected turn when Suma, the 7-year-old bundle of joy, entered the room. Observing the expressions on her uncle and aunt's faces, Suma couldn't help but feel a sense of concern.

"Uncle Vijay and Aunt Vinaya, why do you both look sad? Are little ones, okay?" Suma inquired; her eyes filled with genuine worry.

Vijay and Vinaya exchanged a glance, touched by Suma's perceptiveness. Vinaya, with a tender smile, assured, "Oh, sweetheart, it's not about the babies. We were just talking about something else."

Suma's face brightened as she took a step closer, determination in her eyes. "Don't worry, Uncle and Aunt. I'm going to take really good care of the babies. I won't leave them alone, ever. You don't have to be sad."

Her words, filled with innocence and pure intention, acted like a soothing balm on Vijay and Vinaya's hearts. They hadn't realized the weight of their worries until Suma's comforting assurance lifted the burden.

Vinaya knelt down to Suma's eye level, touched by her sincerity. "Thank you, Suma. Your promise means a lot to us. Knowing that you'll be there for the little ones brings so much comfort."

Vinaya added, "You're going to be the best big sister, Suma. Your love and care will make them feel so special."

Suma beamed with pride, "Of course, Aunt Vinaya! I love the little ones already, and I'll be the best big sister ever!"

The heartwarming interaction among Suma, Vijay, and Vinaya became a poignant testament to the transformative influence of a child's innocence and optimism. It was a gentle force that not only dissipated worries but also kindled a profound sense of hope within the family. Smitha's words, echoing in the couple's minds, planted the seeds of a refreshed commitment to supporting each other through thick and thin. Vijay and Vinaya clung to the shared purpose of building a family, vowing to navigate this turbulent journey hand in hand, with patience as their guiding light.

CHAPTER EIGHTEEN

A Symphony of Sacrifice- Familial Bonds

It's the end of 28th week Vinaya health did not deteriorate further, the medications supported her health. Families unwavering support, stood as pillars of strength beside the couple. Their commitment echoed in every prayer uttered and every shared moment of quiet determination.

The clinic room, illuminated by a sterile glow, resonated with the symphony of sacrifice unfolding in the lives of Vinaya, Vijay, and both their families. Though the air carried the scent of antiseptic, within those walls, emotions surged wildly, unrestrained.

Vinaya lay on the hospital bed, her body a battleground, fighting a silent war against the forces that threatened to snatch away the two lives she cradled within. The weight of sacrifice bore down on her, etching lines of pain on her face, yet in her eyes, there flickered a flame of determination that refused to be extinguished.

As the Doppler echoed through the room, the rhythmic thud of the babies' heartbeat became a lifeline, a fragile melody in the

midst of the storm. Each beat, a testament to the resilience of life, resonated with a mix of desperation and hope that hung heavy in the air.

The family, gathered like soldiers around a wounded comrade, wore their emotions on their sleeves. Tears of relief streamed down the cheeks of Vinaya's mother, her hands clasped in prayer, thanking gods for the tiny victories they celebrated. Vijay, her husband, smiled through the weight of worry, a mask of bravery concealing the fear that lurked beneath.

The gynecologist Priya, a beacon of expertise, brought a ray of hope with each update. "Vinaya's resilience is remarkable," she declared, the relief evident in her voice. Smitha, a pillar of strength for Vinaya, wore a mix of relief and gratitude on her face, realizing the gravity of the decision they had collectively made.

Priya: (To the family) Vinaya's condition is stable, but we need to continue the medications and monitoring. It's crucial to take each day as it comes.

Vinaya's Father: Vinaya, we've been praying for you and the babies. How are you feeling today?

Vinaya: Hmm.... It's a tough journey, Dad, but I can feel the strength from all of you. The babies' heartbeat keeps me going.

Vinaya's Grandmother: You're a brave one, my dear. We're all here for you.

Varun: The doctor said the stability we're seeing is a positive sign. Keep holding on, Vinaya.

Vijay: We're ready, Doctor. We've come this far, and we're not giving up.

Priya: Your collective strength and hope are essential. We'll navigate this together, one day at a time.

In the midst of pain and uncertainty, the family's love became a shield, a source of strength that defied the harsh realities of the hospital room.

Each conversation, laden with extreme emotions, painted a vivid picture of the delicate dance between life's unpredictability and the unyielding bonds of family.

The chapter unfolded with a poignant acknowledgment of the complexities of life and the sacrifices made in the name of love. Amidst the pain and uncertainty, the family clung to the hope that every beat of the Doppler brought them one step closer to the miracle they so fervently prayed for. The story, now etched with the symphony of sacrifice, continued to navigate the delicate dance between life's unpredictable twists and the enduring strength of familial bonds.

59

CHAPTER NINETEEN

MIRACLE IN TENSION

The dawn of the ninth month unfolded like a beacon of hope, the calendar pages turning in sync with the miraculous journey the couple had traversed. As the rays of the morning sun streamed through the clinic's window, it painted the room in hues of relief and joy. The once suffocating tension that had gripped the family now transformed into delicate rays of hope, like the gentle touch of divine hands.

Vijay, a silent warrior in the battle against escalating expenses, managed the financial strain with a resilience that mirrored Vinaya's strength. The calendar, once marked with the daunting 28-week milestone, now became a testament to a journey that defied the odds, a journey laden with sacrifice and unwavering determination.

However, the tranquil atmosphere shattered when the nurse, an unwavering guardian in this saga, noticed fluctuations in the babies' heart rate and Vinaya's blood pressure. The air thickened with tension as the clock mercilessly ticked away. Vinaya, on the sterile bed, faced both pain and anticipation, her face etched with the gravity of the situation.

The once joyful atmosphere transformed into a battlefield of anxiety, the entire family gathering, nervously awaiting news of the impending arrival of their long-awaited grandchildren.

In the midst of the heightened emotions, the doctor's revelation about an emergency C-section cast a panic in the room. Vijay, now grappling not only with financial strain but the imminent danger to his wife and children, faced a surge of worry. The doctor's words cut through the air like a sharp blade, each syllable carrying the weight of a life-altering decision.

Vijay: Doctor, what's happening? Vinaya looks like she's in pain.

Priya: Vijay, we've been closely monitoring Vinaya, and the situation may become critical. Her blood pressure is spiking, and the babies' heart rate is showing signs of distress. We need to act quickly to ensure the safety of both Vinaya and the babies.

Vijay: Is everything going to be, okay?

Priya: Vijay, given the complications, we need to perform an emergency C-section. It's the safest option for both Vinaya and the babies. We're arranging immediate admission to a hospital named "Uthbhavam" which is equipped for such emergencies. We cannot take further risk.

Vijay: Emergency C-section? Ok ok.... What should I do now?

Priya : Vijay, I understand this is overwhelming, but it's the best course of action considering the circumstances. Time is crucial. We want to ensure a smooth delivery and minimize any risks. Call Smitha and inform her; let Varun accompany her.

Vijay: Okay, Doctor. Let's do what's necessary. I just want both Vinaya and the babies to be safe. I am calling them.

The urgency in Vijay's voice mirrored the storm of emotions raging within. The impending emergency C-section plunged the room into a whirlwind of fear and apprehension.

Smitha: We were thinking of calling in the NICU team from "Graceful Beginnings". They are renowned in Mumbai for their expertise. Do you think that's a good idea?

Priya Smitha, that's a proactive and thoughtful approach. If you believe Graceful Beginnings has superior NICU facilities, it might be a good idea to have them on standby for any immediate care the babies might need.

Smitha: We want to ensure that the babies receive the best possible care from the moment they're born. Can you coordinate with the team at Graceful Beginnings?

Priya: Absolutely. I'll make the necessary arrangements and inform the hospital staff about the plan. Having a top-notch NICU team ready is a wise decision.

Smitha: Thank you, Doctor. We just want to be prepared for any scenario. Vinaya and the babies safety is our top priority.

Priya: I appreciate your concern, Smitha. We'll do everything we can to ensure a smooth and safe delivery. I'll get in touch with Graceful Beginnings immediately.

In the operating room, the cold sterility amplified the intensity of the moment.

Vinaya, draped in a sterile gown, clutched Vijay's hand with a grip that conveyed both fear and hope. As the surgeon entered the room, a collective held breath permeated the air.

Vinaya: Vijay, I'm scared.

Vijay: (Squeezing her hand gently) Vinaya, we've been through so much together, and we'll get through this too. The doctors know what they're doing, and we're in good hands.

Vinaya: I just want our babies to be okay.

Vijay: Our babies are going to be just fine. You're so strong, and I'm right here with you. We've waited for this moment for so long and soon we'll be holding our little ones in our arms.

Vinaya: I......I can't wait to see their tiny face.

Vijay: It's going to be the most beautiful moment of our lives. And you, my love, will be an incredible mom.

Vinaya: (Tears in her eyes) Thank you for being here with me, Vijay.

Vijay: Always, Vinaya. We're a team, remember? Now, let's go meet our babies.

As the surgeon initiated the procedure, the room pulsated with a mixture of anxiety and hope. The rhythmic sounds of medical instruments and Vinaya's nervous breaths created a symphony of emotions, an intense backdrop to the life-changing event unfolding.

Surgeon: (To the team) Okay, everyone, let's begin the C-section. Keep me updated on vital signs. Make sure the patient's eyes are covered.

Priya: Vinaya, you're doing great. We'll have your babies in your arms very soon.

Vinaya: Thank you, Doctor. Please take care of our little ones.

Priya: (To Vijay) Vijay, you can sit near Vinaya's head. We'll keep you informed about the progress.

Anesthesiologist: Vinaya try moving your legs.

Vinaya: I can't doctor.

Anesthesiologist: (to the surgeon) we are good to go sir.

Surgeon: (To the team) Scalpel, please. Let's make the incision.

Vijay: (Holding Vinaya's hand) Vinaya, just a little longer. Our babies will be here soon.

Surgeon: (To the team) We're entering the abdominal cavity. All vitals are stable.

Priya: (To Vinaya) You're doing great. Take deep breaths.

Vinaya: I can feel some pressure on my chest.

Surgeon: That's normal, Vinaya. We're making progress.

Anesthesiologist: Vinaya your heart rate is fast, don't panic; take deep breaths.

The atmosphere in the operating room was filled with a mix of tension and excitement as the medical team worked efficiently to bring Vinaya and Vijay's babies into the world. The exchange of words between the medical team created a supportive and reassuring environment during this significant moment of the C-section.

Priya: (To Vinaya) Just a few more moments, and you'll hear your baby's first cry.

Vijay: Vinaya, you're amazing. We're almost there.

Surgeon: (To the team) The amniotic sac is visible. Let's carefully make the incision.

Priya: (To Vinaya) Get ready to meet your little ones, Vinaya.

Vinaya: I can't wait....

Surgeon: (To the team) Baby is out. Cord clamped and cut. (Surgeon going for the second baby ...)

Loud cries pierced through the silence, a beautiful sound that echoed hope and relief. Vinaya and Vijay exchanged tearful smiles as the doctor announced the birth of their babies. The room, once tense, now echoed with the melody of a new life.

Surgeon: A boy and a girl.... Congratulations...

The family waiting outside, their emotions on a rollercoaster ride, erupted in cheers and tears as the news reached them. The atmosphere shifted from the brink of despair to a crescendo of joy, a testament to the resilience of love and the triumph of familial bonds over adversity. The long and arduous journey, marked by sacrifice and uncertainty, now blossomed into a moment of pure bliss as they welcomed the newest members of their family.

CHAPTER TWENTY

HOLDING HOPES

The echoes of medical instruments and hushed conversations created a backdrop for the momentous occasion about to unfold. During the suction the nurse notices a strange coloration in the amniotic fluid. The surgeons, skilled hands moving with practiced precision, were in the final stages of stitching up Vinaya's C-section incision.

Priya: Vinaya, everything is going smoothly. You're doing great.

Vinaya: Thank you, Doctor. Are the babies okay?

Priya Yes, the babies are doing fine. I can hear those adorable cries. Congratulations, you're officially a mom.

Vinaya: (Tears in her eyes) I can't believe it. Thank you for everything.

Priya It's our pleasure, Vinaya. Now, I'm finishing up the stitches. You'll be able to hold your babies soon.

Vinaya: How many stitches?

Priya Just a few more, and we'll be done. You're going to have a tiny scar, but it will fade with time.

Vinaya: As long as both of us are healthy doctor.

Priya: Absolutely, that's the most important thing. You've been so strong throughout this journey.

Vinaya: I had the best team by my side.

Gynecologist: And you have a wonderful family waiting for you. Okay, we're all finished here.

Vinaya: Thank you, Doctor.

As the doctors worked diligently, the anticipation in the room was palpable. Vinaya, under the effect of lower-half anesthesia, anxiously waited to see newborn babies. However, the room's atmosphere shifted dramatically when the pediatrician noticed unexpected changes in both the babies.

Pediatrician: I'm noticing some changes in the babies breathing pattern and skin color. We need to act swiftly.

Nurse: I found some discoloration in the fluid while doing suction.

Surgeon: What's happening, Doctor, Are the babies, okay?

Pediatrician: There are signs of distress. We need the NICU team from Graceful Beginnings here immediately. The babies need specialized care.

Nurse: (On the phone) We need the NICU team to the operating room right away. The babies are showing distress. Are they here yet?

Pediatrician: (To the Surgeon) We can't waste any time. I need oxygen support here, now.

Surgeon: (Directing the team) Everyone, we have a situation. Shift them immediately to our NICU, prepare for the transfer.

Anesthesiologist: I'm making the arrangements. NICU will need space and equipment. I will ask our hospital team to bring the portable incubator.

Nurse: (Speaking into the phone) We need oxygen, incubator and all necessary equipment brought in ASAP.

Pediatrician: (Checking the babies) Let's keep monitoring closely. Until arrangements are done.

Surgeon: (To the team) We have to work efficiently. Get everything ready for the transfer.

Pediatrician: (To the Pediatric Nurse) Stay close to the babies. We're doing everything we can.

The sudden shift in the room was like a storm sweeping through, replacing the joy with an urgent intensity. The medical team, now in crisis mode, demonstrated a seamless coordination of efforts. The impending arrival of the NICU team became a lifeline, and the urgency in their actions reflected the depth of concern for the fragile lives in their hands.

As the NICU team from Graceful Beginnings rushed in, the room buzzed with heightened emotions. The portable incubator was brought in swiftly, and the babies were carefully placed inside for immediate neonatal care. The once celebratory atmosphere now tinged with anxiety and fear, as the medical team worked fervently to stabilize the newborn.

Pediatrician: (To the Pediatric Nurse) Let's ensure a smooth transfer. Every second counts.

Nurse: I'm right here, Doctor.

The atmosphere, once filled with the scent of hope, now held the weight of uncertainty. The room, once echoing with cries of joy, now hummed with a tense symphony of medical urgency.

The NICU team, experts in their field, began their delicate dance to ensure the precious life entrusted to them would receive the best possible care.

In the midst of this chaotic scene, Vinaya, recovering from the intensity of childbirth, could only watch with a heart full of anxiety and a silent prayer on her lips. The rollercoaster of emotions had taken an unexpected turn, and the journey that began with the promise of new life now faced a critical juncture, where the skill and expertise of the medical team would determine the fate of the fragile newborns.

In the urgency of the NICU, the medical team moved with precision, and the pediatrician maintained a constant dialogue with Vinaya, updating her on the relentless efforts being made to ensure the well-being of her precious babies. The room buzzed with intensity as each member of the team played a crucial role in the dramatic endeavor to care for the newborns.

Vinaya: Doctor, please make sure our babies are okay. I can't bear not knowing.

Pediatrician: We understand your concern, Vinaya. Our priority is the well-being of your babies. We'll do everything in our power to ensure a positive outcome.

The minutes felt like an eternity as Vinaya, helpless on the operating table, clung to the hope that the NICU team's expertise would guide her newborn through this crucial phase. The room, once filled with tears of joy, was now heavy with the collective worry of the medical team and the family waiting anxiously outside.

The pediatrician, though focused on the task at hand, recognized the need for reassurance and support. Amidst the urgency, a sense of compassion emanated from the medical team as they navigated the delicate balance between professional responsibility and the raw emotions of a family facing an unexpected ordeal.

Pediatrician: Vinaya, the babies are responding well to the interventions. We're stabilizing the condition. We'll keep monitoring closely.

Vinaya: Thank you, Doctor. Please take good care of our babies.

Pediatrician: That's our commitment, Vinaya. Your babies are in good hands. We'll update you as soon as there's more information.

The room, once engulfed in anxiety, now held a flicker of hope. The NICU team, with their expertise and dedication, became the beacon guiding the family through this unforeseen storm. Vinaya, though physically separated from her newborns, drew strength from the reassurance of the pediatrician and the knowledge that every effort was being made to ensure the babies well-being.

Outside the operating room, the family, previously jubilant, now clung to each other, their faces a mosaic of worry and anticipation. Smitha, Varun, and Vijay exchanged glances, their unspoken support a silent acknowledgment of the challenges that lay ahead. The waiting room, once filled with joyous expectations, now echoed with the palpable tension of an uncertain future.

CHAPTER TWENTY-ONE

A Fragile Beginning

Once they had stabilized both the babies, the air in the neonatal care unit thickened with the weight of anticipation. The team of doctors moved with a choreographed precision, wheeling the portable incubator into the ambulance bound for Graceful Beginnings hospital. Inside, two fragile souls lay, pale and delicate, in need of the tender care only medical experts could provide. The soft hum of oxygen support echoed the collective heartbeat of the family, who eagerly awaited the sight of the newborn and his mother.

The family, an abstract canvas painting of worry and hope, gathered in a hushed silence, their eyes revealing a mix of curiosity and concern. A palette of emotions played across their faces as they braced themselves for a glimpse of the fragile newcomers who are about to embark on their journey to the neonatal hospital.

As the portable incubator was carefully positioned, allowing the family a momentary view, a wave of emotion swept through the room. The babies were small, vulnerable, yet embodied a symbol of hope and tenacity.

Murmurs of concern intertwined with whispers of support as the family stared at the fragile form within.

Vinaya's Mother, her voice barely audible: "Look at them, so tiny in that incubator. Are they okay?"

Smitha, speaking softly: "The pediatrician said they're monitoring them closely. Let's stay positive."

Vinaya's Father, his voice filled with prayer: "Our little warriors. He's going to pull through, I can feel it."

Vijay, watching intently: "They so small, but they look strong. Our little fighters."

Vinaya's Grandmother, blessing from a distance: "Don't worry, my dear. They are in good hands. We just need to have faith."

Varun, reassuring the family: "The NICU team from Graceful Beginnings is top-notch. They getting the best care."

Smitha, noticing the babies' movements: "Look, they are moving his little hands".

Vijay, addressing the family: "We're all here for them. They'll have the strongest support system."

The family, though filled with worry, found solace in the sight of the babies in the incubator. Their collective hope and support created a cocoon of love around the fragile newborns as they began their journey to the neonatal hospital. The whispered conversations echoed both concern and optimism, painting together a landscape of emotions that marked the beginning of a new chapter for the family.

The Ambulance Driver interjected with a practical reminder: "We have limited space in the ambulance. Only one person can accompany us for now."

Vijay, looking at Varun: "I'll go with the babies. You can follow us in the Car."

Smitha, nodding: "Alright, Vijay. We'll stay close."

Vijay, to the driver: "Thank you. Let's get going. We'll be right behind you in the Car."

Ambulance Driver: "Sure. We're heading to Graceful Beginnings NICU. The doctors will be closely monitoring the child during the journey."

Smitha, calling after Vijay: "Vijay, keep us updated. We'll be right there."

Varun, with a hand on Smitha's shoulder: "Don't worry, Smitha. We'll follow them safely."

Smitha, nervously smiling: "Yeah. Everything will be alright."

As Vijay boarded the ambulance, Smitha watched with a mix of anxiety and determination. Varun and Smitha quickly prepared to follow the ambulance in their car, ensuring they stayed close during this crucial journey to Graceful Beginnings NICU.

The family's support extended beyond the hospital walls, and the coordination between the brothers exemplified their commitment to being there for the babies and the rest of the family.

Vijay, his brother Varun, and Smitha embarked on the journey to the neonatal hospital, their hearts heavy with concern for the newest member of the family. Manju and other relatives stood outside the ICU; their collective breaths held as they waited for Vinaya's return.

Inside the neonatal care unit, the doctors meticulously tended to the newborns. His pallor spoke volumes of the challenges that lay ahead. Meanwhile, Vinaya's situation, unknown to those in the neonatal care unit, was being addressed by a team of diligent doctors at Uthbhavam. Her swellings had miraculously reduced.

The need for Vinaya's observation for the next 24 hours was emphasized as she was shifted to ICU for recovery. The family, though anxious, understood the importance of this critical period.

The doctors assured them that once the observation period was complete, Vinaya would be shifted to a general room.

The intensity of emotions continued to surge as the family braced themselves for the unfolding chapters of this delicate and fragile beginning.

CHAPTER TWENTY-TWO

WHISPERS OF RESILIENCE

Vijay, Varun, and Smitha paced the sterile corridors outside the Neonatal Intensive Care Unit (NICU), their hearts weighed down by the uncertainty that loomed over the fragile newborns within. The air felt suffocating as they awaited news, their collective anxiety palpable in the sterile environment.

The doctors emerged from the NICU, their faces a delicate dance of caution and compassion, carrying with them the weight of the fragile lives they were entrusted to care for. In a quiet consultation room adjacent to the NICU, the medical team gently unraveled the reality of their condition.

The Doctor, choosing his words carefully: "Vijay, Smitha, Varun, I appreciate your understanding during this critical time. I want to be transparent with you about possible conditions the newborns may face due to distress."

Vijay, his voice tense but determined: "Please, tell us what we need to know. We want to be prepared."

The Doctor continued, laying out potential challenges with a gravity that hung in the air like a storm cloud. Smitha, nervously biting her lip, sought answers about the babies' potential issues, her worry etched on her face like a deep scar.

Doctor: "Given to the situation in which they were born, we'll also be vigilant for signs of irregular breathing. Our team is well-equipped to monitor and address any complications. We will also check his vital organs. Just to be sure. To confirm we need to do scans and X-rays."

Varun, his concern etched across his features: "Ok, Doctor. What should we do from our end?"

Doctor: "Your support is crucial. Understand that we're taking every precaution and have the best specialists available. The NICU at Graceful Beginnings is equipped to handle these situations. We will do everything in our power to keep them safe."

Vijay, taking a deep breath that echoed the weight of the moment: "Thank you for being honest with us, Doctor."

The doctor's candid explanation, while delivering potentially difficult information, aimed to empower Vijay, Smitha, and Varun as caregivers. Transparency about potential issues, coupled with the reassurance of a dedicated medical team, is crucial in fostering trust and collaboration during such delicate circumstances.

Smitha, her voice laced with concern: "Doctor, I was wondering about their feeding. What should we expect in terms of nutrition for them?"

Doctor: "Smitha, we've already made arrangements for neonatal feed in the NICU. Our team is experienced in providing specialized nutrition for them. We'll initiate the feeding process in accordance with their condition."

Smitha, relieved but still anxious: "That's reassuring. Is there anything specific we need to know or do?"

Doctor: "Right now, it's crucial to give the mother, Vinaya, some time to recover. Vinaya needs rest and care to regain her strength."

Smitha, with a heartfelt sigh: "Of course, we want Vinaya to recover well. Thank you for explaining, Doctor. We just want to make sure we're doing everything we can to support both Vinaya and the babies."

Doctor: "Your support is invaluable, Smitha. We'll keep you informed about their progress, and once Vinaya is ready, she can also participate in caring for the babies,

Smitha, with determination in her voice: "That sounds good. We'll be here every step of the way."

The conversation between Smitha and the doctor highlighted the importance of understanding the babies nutritional needs and the need for Vinaya's recovery. The doctor's reassurance and guidance provided Smitha with a sense of clarity, allowing her to actively contribute to the care and support of both Vinaya and the newborns during this critical time.

The Doctor, breaking the tension: "Please proceed to the first floor, provide the details, and the admin team will speak to you about the estimated cost."

The chapter unfolded with the realization that life, with its stories of unexpected beginnings and uncharted paths, was a turbulent sea of emotions. The family, though shaken by the fragility of the present, clung to the hope that whispered in the corridors of the NICU. The newborns, tiny beacon of strength, lay in the embrace of modern medicine, family support, and the unwavering spirit of resilience that would guide them through the challenging days that lay ahead. The atmosphere resonated with a symphony of intense emotions, ranging from fear to determination, and from uncertainty to a flicker of hope that refused to be extinguished.

CHAPTER TWENTY-THREE

MEDICAL REVELATION

Vijay sat on the edge of his seat, anxiety gnawing at him, awaiting the pediatrician's verdict on the test results. The air in the room hung thick with tension as the doctor entered, clutching a folder that contained the crucial reports. The weight of the impending news pressed down on Vijay, the specter of the unknown casting a dark shadow over him.

The pediatrician, with a solemn demeanor, began to explain the delicate situation. Each word felt like a heavy blow, sinking Vijay deeper into a sea of worry. The cost, an ever-present specter, loomed large over him, threatening to swallow any semblance of reassurance. The hospital's restrictions, limiting parental visits and enforcing stringent infection control measures in the NICU, added a layer of complexity to an already intricate and emotionally charged situation.

Pediatrician: "Mr. Vijay, I've reviewed the X-rays and scans. I need to discuss the findings with you."

Vijay, his voice quivering with nerves: "Please, doctor, tell me what's going on. Are they, okay?"

Pediatrician: "Mr. Vijay, I understand this is a challenging time for you. We've identified Meconium Aspiration Syndrome (MAS) based on the tests we conducted."

Vijay, anxiety etched across his face: "MAS? What does that mean for our babies?"

Pediatrician: "Meconium is the baby's first stool, and in some cases, it can be passed into the amniotic fluid. If the baby inhales or aspirates this meconium into the lungs, it can lead to respiratory issues, which is what we suspect has happened."

Vijay, his worry intensifying: "What are the potential complications we should be prepared for?"

Pediatrician: "MAS can cause inflammation in the lungs, and in severe cases, it may result in pneumonia. However, I want to assure you that we have a dedicated team in the Neonatal

Intensive Care Unit (NICU) providing the best possible care for your babies."

Vijay, concern deepening: "How serious is the situation?"

Pediatrician: "We're closely monitoring both the babies' respiratory function. Right now, our priority is to provide respiratory support and ensure both of them receive enough oxygen. The NICU team is doing everything they can to prevent complications."

Vijay, nodding with a heavy heart: "What's the treatment plan moving forward?"

Pediatrician: "We'll continue the respiratory support, closely observing your babies progress. We'll keep you updated on any developments, and we appreciate your patience during this critical period."

Vijay, visibly overwhelmed, absorbed the pediatrician's words, each piece of information hitting him with the force of a tidal wave.

At Uthbhavam Hospital, the family found solace in the whispers of resilience that echoed through their shared glances as they waited for Vinaya's recovery. Each detailed conversation that Vijay had with the pediatrician provided a roadmap for the days ahead; a lifeline reassuring them that both the newborns are receiving the best care possible in the pursuit of a healthy and hopeful future. The extremes of emotions, from paralyzing fear to a flicker of hope, danced in the air, creating a symphony of heart-wrenching intensity that defined this crucial chapter in their lives.

CHAPTER TWENTY-FOUR

FINANCIAL PRESSURE

Vijay, trapped in the hurricane of emotions, stood at the precipice where joy and challenge collided. The doctors, clad in white coats and grave expressions, presented him with a stark duality—the bliss of welcoming new lives interwoven with the daunting task of traversing the uncharted territory of medical complexities.

Overwhelmed and lost in the labyrinth of responsibilities, Vijay questioned his ability to manage everything. "How am I going to handle all of this?" In his moment of despair, Varun, the unwavering pillar of support, stepped forward with a promise that cut through the darkness like a beacon of hope. "We are there; we will help," he whispered, a vow that resonated with the unyielding strength of familial solidarity. Together, they faced the hospital's insurance department, seeking a lifeline amidst the bureaucratic maze of healthcare.

Admin Team: Mr. Vijay, please come in. We understand this is a challenging time for your family, and we're here to assist you with the financial aspects.

Vijay: Thank you. We appreciate your help.

Admin Team: First, let's go over the estimated cost for the initial days in the NICU. Considering the specialized care required, the total comes to around 10 lakhs.

Vijay, feeling a nerve-racking tremor, reflected, "During the past Four months from the 6th to the 9th month of Vinaya's pregnancy, we had to stay in the hospital, facing escalating expenses and other hospital charges. Now, an additional ten lakhs! How will I manage?"

Admin Team: We understand the financial strain this might cause. Now, regarding insurance coverage; your wife's health insurance policy is expected to cover approximately 60% of the total cost of NICU.

Vijay, a sigh of relief escaping him: "That's helpful. What about the remaining 40%?"

Admin Team: We have options for payment plans and financial assistance. Our team is here to guide you through the process, and we'll work closely with you to ensure the best possible support.

Vijay, grateful for the lifeline: "Thank you for being considerate. Can you break down the insurance coverage for a better understanding?"

Admin Team: Certainly. The insurance is expected to cover medical procedures, diagnostics, and a portion of the NICU stay. However, certain medications and additional services might have separate coverage or require co-payments.

Vijay, pen in hand, taking notes with a determination in his eyes: "Got it. We want the best for our babies, so we'll do whatever it takes. What's the next step?"

Admin Team: Please fill out these forms with your details. Once completed, we'll schedule a meeting with our financial counselor to discuss the payment plans and explore any available assistance programs.

Vijay, resolute in his purpose: "Thank you. We'll get this done promptly. We just want to focus on our babies' well-being."

Admin Team: Absolutely, Mr. Vijay. We're here to support you every step of the way. The team of doctors has informed us that the babies might need 15 days of intensive care.

The news of 15 days of intensive care cast a shadow over the family, their hearts burdened by the impending journey that awaited the tiny warriors in the NICU.

Varun, embodying the spirit of brotherhood, consoled Vijay. "Things will work for us; don't worry," he affirmed, offering a steadying hand in the turbulent sea of uncertainty. With the paperwork set in motion, they embarked to meet Vinaya, each step echoing with a collective determination to face the challenges ahead.

The chapter unfolded as a symphony of extreme emotions, showcasing the resilience of familial bonds and the courage found in the face of unforeseen trials.

As Vijay and Varun navigated the intricacies of the hospital's financial uncertainties, they clung to the belief that, together, they could weather the storm and emerge on the other side with a story of triumph against the odds. The air crackled with the intensity of their emotions—fear, hope, and the unwavering spirit that bound them as a family.

CHAPTER TWENTY-FIVE

"THE RADIANT DAWN OF HOPE"

In the quaint pages of their life, Vijay and Vinaya found themselves entwined in a chapter titled: "The Radiant Dawn of Hope". The words unfolded slowly, each sentence laden with anticipation and anxiety. The family, the radiant colors of support, stood resiliently beside them, weaving threads of hope in the intricate narrative of their journey.

As Vinaya recuperated in the hospital, the medical team provided meticulous care, transforming the sterile walls into a sanctuary of productive healing. She got discharged from the hospital and it's time for her to visit gynecologist again to remove the knots from the stitches made.

Vinaya: Vijay, I have the post-discharge checkup with my gynecologist today. Would you be able to accompany me?

Vijay: Of course, Vinaya. I'll make sure we get there on time. How are you feeling?

Vinaya: Much better, actually. The hospital stay did wonders, and I can't wait to have these stitches removed.

Vijay: It's amazing how quickly you're recovering. The doctor did mention you're progressing well.

Vinaya: Yeah, it's a relief. I'm eager to get back to normal routines and take care of our little ones. I know you have been updating me about our little ones. It's time, I want to go and hold them in my arms.

Vijay: Speaking of which, they doing great; the doctors are pleased with their progress in the NICU.

Vinaya: (Gently touching Vijay's hand) That's the best news. Let's focus on making sure both of us are in top shape for when they come home.

Vijay: Absolutely. We're almost there. Once you're done with the checkup, maybe we can treat ourselves to something nice.

Vinaya: Oh! Yeah,I like the sound of that.

Vijay: It's a plan, then. Let's head to the gynecologist and then make the most of our day.

As they embark on the journey to the gynecologist's office, Vijay and Vinaya share a moment of quiet optimism. The checkup marks another step towards normalcy, and the prospect of having the knots removed is a symbolic gesture of healing. Together, they navigate the delicate balance of recovery and anticipation, looking forward to the day when their little ones join them at home.

In the quiet hum of the NICU, the babies' journey mirrored that of a delicate butterfly emerging from a cocoon. The hospital, a haven of expertise, became the nurturing ground for their tiny miracles. The alarms that once echoed with uncertainty transformed into the soothing lullabies of monitors indicating stability.

As they celebrate Vijay receives a call from Graceful Beginnings.

Doctor: Vijay, I'm pleased to inform you that after 10 days, of dedicated care, your babies are ready to be discharged from the hospital. We initially thought it might extend to 15days or so. As they quickly progressed, it's time for them to go home.

Vijay: That's incredible news! We've been waiting for this day. How are they doing?

Doctor: Both the babies made remarkable progress during their time in the NICU. Their vital signs are stable, and they reached a point where they can continue their growth and development in the comfort of your home.

Vijay: Thank you so much, Doctor. We can't express how much we are grateful to the team...

Doctor: It's been our pleasure to be a part of this journey. Now, as they are coming home, there will be some guidelines and instructions to follow. We'll provide you with all the necessary information and ensure a smooth transition.

Vijay: Absolutely, we'll follow every advice of yours. When can we take them home?

Doctor: Tomorrow morning. We want to make sure everything is in order and that you feel comfortable with the care routine. Our nurses will walk you through any special considerations.

Vijay: (Smiling) Tomorrow it is, then. We can't wait to have them home.

Doctor: Take this time to prepare, Vijay. And don't hesitate to ask any questions. We're here to support you even after the discharge.

Vijay: Thank you, Doctor. Your unwavering dedication and expertise have been our guiding light. As we embark on this new chapter, we are truly grateful for the care and support you've provided. The long wait has been filled with both hope and apprehension, and we can't wait to share this joyous news with my wife. Your efforts have made a profound impact on our lives, and for that, we are forever thankful."

Vinaya: What happened Vijay? You seem to be happy? What is happening tomorrow?

Vijay: Our babies are coming home. Yay!......(Couple warmly shares a hug)

The much-anticipated arrival of the babies is just a few hours away. The couple's journey of love, care, and overcoming challenges is now unfolding into a beautiful new chapter in their lives.

CHAPTER TWENTY-SIX

"REUNION OF HEARTS"

Eleven days had unfolded like an eternity for Vinaya, each moment a yearning for the touch of her newborns. The separation, a poignant ache, reverberated through the sterile hospital corridors. Today, the long-awaited moment had arrived. The nurse carefully placed them in Vinaya's arms, and as their eyes met, a symphony of emotions played in the silent room.

Vinaya whispers; Hello, my little ones. I've been waiting for you.

Cradling her babies, Vinaya felt the delicate weight of tiny fingers, counting each one, committing the moment to memory. The room seemed to fade away, leaving only the tender connection between mother and her childern.

Vinaya: Oh my God.... Both of you are perfect in every way.

The babies, nestled in the warmth of Vinaya's embrace, stirred as if recognizing the familiar heartbeat they had accompanied for months.

Vinaya: (Gently kissing her babies forehead) I missed you, my darling. These eleven days felt like an eternity.

The separation, though brief, had left an indelible mark on Vinaya's heart. The sleepless nights, the yearning glances toward the nursery, and the quiet conversations with the moonlit sky—all moments leading to this reunion.

Nurse: It's a beautiful sight, isn't it? Mother and her children, finally together.

Vinaya: (Nodding with tears in her eyes) It's more beautiful than I could have ever imagined.

In a room once filled with the hum of medical equipment, the atmosphere now echoed with the lullaby of a mother's whispered words and the soft coos of her newborns.

The journey, filled with uncertainties and challenges, had brought them to this profound moment of union. As this connection blossomed, a warm flow of milk erupted from her bosom.

Vinaya: (Looking at the nurse) Thank you for taking care of my little ones.

Nurse: It's our pleasure. We're here to ensure both of you are healthy and happy.

As the nurse left the room, Vinaya continued to revel in the joy of holding her children, their hearts beating in unison. Vinaya, cradling her newborns, knew that the days ahead would be a journey of discovery, love, and the unbreakable bond between a mother and her child.

As Vijay completes impending discharge duties, emotions of joy and gratitude fill the room. The doctor's assurance and guidance provide comfort to Vijay, who eagerly awaits the moment when he can bring his little ones home after eleven days of meticulous care in the hospital.

The family, once shadowed by hardships, became pillars of strength, embracing the wait with grace. Each visit to the hospital was a lesson in patience and resilience. Vijay, with unwavering determination, balanced the roles of a supportive partner and a new father with grace, learning the delicate dance of parenthood.

Vinaya's Mother: Vijay, you've been such a rock through all of this. Your determination is inspiring.

Vijay: Thank you, Aunty. We're in this together. Every day, I see our little ones getting stronger, and it gives me hope.

Vijay's Father: (Patting Vijay's back) You're doing an excellent job, son. Parenthood is a journey of its own, and you're handling it with grace.

Vijay: I appreciate that. Vinaya and I are learning as we go. It's a beautiful journey, albeit with its challenges.

Vinaya's Grandmother: Every challenge makes you stronger, my dear. These hardships will become stories to tell your little ones someday.

Vijay: I believe that. And we're surrounded by such a supportive family. Your presence has made all the difference.

Manju: To strength, resilience, and the unwavering support of family. We've weathered the storm together, and now, we celebrate the imminent arrival of joy.

As Suma delicately touched the babies, her eyes lit up with a mixture of awe and tenderness. "Hello, my baby brother and sister," she whispered with a soft giggle. "I am going to take good care of you."

She gently nuzzled the babies and took in a deep breath. "Hmm, you both smell good. I am Suma, your sister. Don't worry; if you need anything, you can ask me, okay?"

The sweet exchange between Suma and the newborns radiated love and affection.

The family, witnessing this heartwarming moment, couldn't help but burst into laughter. The air was filled with joy as Suma's promises and endearing words created a bond that transcended words.

Everyone: Laughter echoed. (There were celebrations in the family.)

In the midst of hardship, the family finds joy in the resilience they've discovered within themselves. The happy conversations echo with the shared triumphs and the anticipation of welcoming the babies into their loving embrace. The extended wait wasn't just a passage of time; it unfolded as a transformative chapter that added depth to the narrative of their lives.

Vijay, with a sense of gravity, handed over a sealed note to Vinaya. "Keep this note safe," he whispered, his eyes filled with a mix of anticipation and emotion. "I want you to give this to our son and daughter when they turn 18 years old."

The atmosphere hung heavy with unspoken sentiments, as if the note held secrets and wisdom meant to be unveiled at a future juncture. The exchange carried the weight of a promise, a piece of their shared journey destined to be revealed to their children when the time was ripe with significance.

Vinaya: What is this?

Vijay: "A Heartfelt Note."

Their life's experiences were more than mere passages of time; each trial and triumph became a story, not just for personal growth but as tales meant to be shared—an offering of insights for others to gain wisdom from.

As this chapter of their journey concluded, it carried a sense of closure, akin to the final scene in a play where characters take a bow. The lessons, challenges, and victories would now linger as stories, ready to inspire and guide those who would follow. The chapter may have ended, but its echoes remained, poised to resonate in the hearts and minds of those who would listen.

The End

A Message To The Readers

As the novel comes to an end, the stage is bathed in a warm, golden glow. Vinaya and Vijay stand together, transformed by the crucible of life's struggles. Their journey, though marked by pain and adversity, is a testament to the transformative power of resilience and love.

Life, a grand drama with its share of challenges, becomes a canvas upon which we paint our stories of triumph. Vinaya and Vijay's tale reminds us that it is not the absence of struggles that defines us but rather how we learn, adapt, and emerge stronger in the face of adversity. In the grand theatre of life, their story becomes an enduring narrative of hope—a beacon for others facing their own trials.

And so, the novel ends, leaving the audience with a profound message: Life's struggles are the crucible in which we are refined, and it is in overcoming them that our truest selves are revealed.

www.ingramcontent.com/pod-product-compliance
Lightning Source LLC
Chambersburg PA
CBHW021114130726
47988CB00003B/1021